Lee is a tattoo artist and writer of surreal urban fantasy, living and working in Northumberland. A father of three, keen fitness enthusiast, retro gamer and an avid reader of an extensive range of fiction. Lee lives alone to better immerse himself in the abject solitude required to conjure such a stew of cerebral nightmares.

Tripper Treadmore and the Bloodsuckers from Maddison and French is dedicated to my late mother who died during its writing, and no doubt my spiking emotions and anxieties would have flavoured its passages.

I'd like to imagine, therefore, that readers can share in my distresses, and maybe lighten their burden awhile.

Lee Short

THE OLDEST SOAK

and other weird tales

AUSTIN MACAULEY PUBLISHERS™
LONDON • CAMBRIDGE • NEW YORK • SHARJAH

Copyright © Lee Short 2022

The right of Lee Short to be identified as author of this work has been asserted by the author in accordance with sections 77 and 78 of the Copyright, Designs and Patents Act 1988.

All rights reserved. No part of this publication may be reproduced, stored in a retrieval system, or transmitted in any form or by any means, electronic, mechanical, photocopying, recording, or otherwise, without the prior permission of the publishers.

Any person who commits any unauthorised act in relation to this publication may be liable to criminal prosecution and civil claims for damages.

This is a work of fiction. Names, characters, businesses, places, events, locales, and incidents are either the products of the author's imagination or used in a fictitious manner. Any resemblance to actual persons, living or dead, or actual events is purely coincidental.

A CIP catalogue record for this title is available from the British Library.

ISBN 9781398444461 (Paperback)
ISBN 9781398444478 (ePub e-book)

www.austinmacauley.com

First Published 2022
Austin Macauley Publishers Ltd®
1 Canada Square
Canary Wharf
London
E14 5AA

Table of contents

Scott's Got One Kidney   9
(The Dissolution of Mikie Bircham)

Aces   20
(Soldiers in the Fields)

The Urban Legend of Geordie-Pop   29
(Eulogy for Holy Field)

The Oldest Soak   40
(What's the Score with Teas, Dale?)

Tripper Treadmore and the Bloodsuckers from Maddison and French   60
(Coal-Black Limousine)

Mind Porridge   76
(An Introduction to the New Normal)

Pepper Siege Three   89
(The Short Flare)

Look at Your Game   111
(The Conjected Inauguration of Animal Strap)

Rue de la Châtaigne   127
(The Loss of Innocence)

Layten's Chute   146
(Those Likely Boys)

The Cat Hits Back

(No-One Cares, Work Harder)

Scott's Got One Kidney
(The Dissolution of Mikie Bircham)

High above the cold, mulberry waves of the North Sea, I secluded in my windy folly, far from the prying eyes of the general public and their I interfering ways. Being blessed of considerable financial stature, I was able to pursue the life of a recluse, such as my dark past had sadly dictated. As each desolate morning shone its unwelcome beam through my windows, ushering in another day filled with untapped potential and opportunity for glory, so did my face wrinkle and my spine bow under the unbearable burden of guilt that had settled on my bony shoulders. So great was my single crime that its lament had driven me insane, the black tumour of anticipated penance chomping away at my limited vitality until what remained was an imitation of man. The crooked, wounded figure that limped daily from room to room to sustain its miserable existence held a zest comparable to that of the rotten sea lion carcass that bounced upon the frothy waves, butting against the rocks on the day I threw Scott's accursed pink kidney from my kitchen window.

Wholly undeserving of the sinister twist of fate that befell him, was Scott. A gentle, smiling ox of a man, he'd ne'er a salty word for anyone. With colossal beef shoulders and a huge red beard as though all of autumn had clustered about his chin, he projected a formidable persona, yet his tiny eyes betrayed a glad soul that would share his last bean with no consideration of reward or recompense.

So what drove me to such dismal lunacy as to conspire to remove his kidney? Across the weeks and months since that deeply regretful and irrevocable evening that very question has tormented me like an awful rat, nibbling at the ragged shreds of my sanity with infected mandibles. In all honesty, that night I was possessed of an unusually overwhelming compulsion, during which my gluttonous yearning for scientific excellence held dominance over all my ethics and principles. The covert and unlawful procurement of one of Scott's kidneys was simply an experiment to clarify whether it could be done, and results were *partially* successful.

For years an aspiring human biologist, I won't deny I considered the eccentric image of a renegade surgeon to be medicine's answer to rock and roll stardom, and studied fastidiously, far beyond the capabilities of my fellow medics. Much to the chagrin of my industriously handicapped tutors, I persisted in attempting to facilitate a mode of expedience within the current curriculum, which I found to be a most tedious and drawn-out affair. Despite my avaricious efforts, the scholastic body remained defiant in the face of my enthusiasm, and so my learnings were incurred at a snail's pace. Astonishing that even in this modern age, individual excellence was discouraged in favour of a tightly controllable, uniform collective.

Bosom buddies, Scott and I had often taken full advantage of my remote location to indulge in the brash consumption of all things illicit and unlawful, specifically (and ordinarily) drugs and sluts, and it seemed inevitable that the presence of one guaranteed the advent of the other. A regular favourite within our degenerate inner-city menu had been the in-house preparation of mescaline tea, brewed from the multiple clusters of unassuming peyote cacti that graced the dusty alabaster nooks of my home. From the comfort of the snug we had embarked on epic journeys to the far reaches of experience and witnessed enlightening distortions of time and matter such as the average mortal man will never know the like. Such had been the extent of our habitually nefarious conduct that the accumulation of liquor bottles, soiled needles and spent prophylactics weighed not one whit against my unwavering levity. Indeed, their presence merely compounded the attitude with which I chose to affront modern society and all its muted, infuriating regularities.

And so it *needles* to me to confess that during one such overindulgence, I anaesthetised my overgrown friend and promptly performed an unlawful backyard nephrectomy. Fortunately for myself, I was able to detain him during a rather surreal recovery period of one week, aided by the furtive administration of granulated morphine and a whole lot of gingerly applied bullshit. Due in no small part to his narcotised condition, I easily convinced Scott that his residual discomfort was the direct result of our heroin use and was able to legitimately empathise. It was only once he'd departed to reintegrate with the world that the sheer gravity of my woeful transgression fell upon me like an unmerciful iceberg, bristling with all manner of contaminated sharps, and coated with salt.

Thus began a period of deepest, darkest self-loathing and rumination, during which my brilliant scientific mind was mother to an astonishing medley of projected outcomes to this terribly revolting episode of my inception. I won't deny that during this difficult time I became unhinged and considered that the only means to quell my anxieties was to leap from an upper storey, dashing my tortured *mind-case* on the goring rocks below. The merciful tide would then concede to dispel my woes as they frothed from my cracked skull, nourishing the plankton in a final, honourable gesture of atonement. As it were, the self-righteous smile of Scott's neat nephrectomy scar haunted my every waking moment, and indeed, my dreams were even worse.

An unknown matter of days since I relented to allow Scott his freedom, (the calendar had so little bearing on my existence now that the passage of time had been reduced to a cursory acknowledgement of dark and light spells) I was paid a visit by his elder brother, Big Jim. Constructed according to a very similar mould to Scott, Big Jim's prodigious fist beat upon my door with the dull assertion of a policeman wielding a "big red key." Upon recognition of his firm, jutting chin, my heart underwent a seismic palpitation that blew the cobwebs from my arms and set my fingertips to throb most uncharacteristically.

It was my opinion at this juncture, that should Big Jim's intention be the reconstitution of my vertebrae into a new and unusual configuration, then at least that brief flare of agonizing pain and shameful acknowledgement of my skulduggery would spell an end to the corrosive anxieties I was inflicting on my own psyche daily. Armed with this new resolve, I approached the stoop as a convicted felon contemplating the gibbet.

"Good morning, James," I offered, my wavering voice betraying the fear that was turning my formerly solid stools into a thin and unpleasant gravy.

"Hey, Mikie," he refreshingly reciprocated.

Thrown by his light, dispassionate tone, my brain was a maelstrom of jumbled responses and conflicting emotions. Was it then conceivable that Scott's urinary downgrade remained a precarious and potentially damning secret? By the very nature of my awkward hesitation I was picking at its metaphorical scab, and thus encouraging the cultivation of a more pronounced and discoverable scar.

"Good to see you, James," I bantered. "What is it I can do for you?"

"Nothin'," he conceded. "Just figured I'd drop by. Blowin' in the wind, y'know?"

Under the provisional assumption that there had been recent social contact between Big Jim and his brother, it appeared that I had been accorded an amnesty, and therefore Scott was effecting a remarkable recovery. Nevertheless, my ravaged nerves were manifest, and Big Jim's dismissal seemed crucial if this abominable subterfuge were to be sustained.

"If it's all the same, I've rather a lot on, mate," I replied.

"Hey, no problem," he answered. "Nobody's seen you in a while, is all."

"Yeah, I'm just kinda taking a break from life," I lied. "Basking in the solitude, you know how it is."

Spurning Big Jim's proffered social interaction, I detected a fleeting shadow of rejection sullying the typically buoyant contours of his face.

"I guess we'll see you around some time, then," he suggested.

"I'm pretty sure you will," I added, daringly. "In one capacity or another."

"Later, man."

Awash with relief at Big Jim's departure and salubrious ignorance, I withdrew to the familiarities of my shadowy lair to further immerse myself in the dubious comfort of my private miseries. Whilst reclining with my demons I sank into a haunted sleep, menaced by thoughts of the dolphin-smooth human organ that previously nestled in my kitchen drawer above stairs, and the potential discovery of its absence from Scott's posterior. Surely the very notion of a misappropriated kidney was such a monumentally ludicrous proposition that its suspicion should never arise, yet its phantom goaded me from among the drawing pins, screwdrivers and nonmatching dice. Through superfluous pizza-shop menus and across chequered tiles it wept, its soft sob accusing and tragic like the sea.

The infinite ocean, deeply cold of heart and of caress.

Pulse of the world, perpetual marauder and palace of mysteries and wonder.

Its ebb and flow striking tallies of woe upon my face.

As it chews of the pocked and rasping stones, so does its tireless choir erode my will until the day its winds fetch fat flies to lay maggots in my traitor belly.

Then will it whisper of triumph and justice, but fleetingly.

As it shall again buoy children and raise fishes for the hungry.

Again, a pounding at my door, as of gluttonous hands clawing at what little I still held. By the length of my gnarled and tarnished fingernails, was I safe in assuming this was a later date than that which had engendered Big Jim's visit, or was my brooding plumbing new depths, inclusive of maudlin self-sacrifice? These were indeed dangerous times, when a man cared so little for his own fare that every neat little cell on my formerly exhausting year planner was simply a formal division of the night, during which I could better see my own debilitating shortcomings. Once more, the door; a loathsome encore to deplore, and another chore to be sure.

Atop my weed-riddled stoop there loitered an arguably attractive lady by the name of Lacey Beenshill. A former lover of a very casual bent, she was unaware of my current attentions from behind dappled glass and gazed disinterestedly around my neglected garden. Despite my odious reek and dishevelled appearance, I opined that I'd be more prominent in my absence, especially if the news were to be collated with my unusual lack of interest in the fortunes and fare of Big Jim. With crackling tendons and accompanying tremors of indefinite origin, I threw wide my door.

"Wow," Lacey blurted, as her predatory eyes fed greedily of my lowly aesthetic. "What the Christ happened to you?"

"I'm taking a leave of absence," I fumbled. "What's your excuse?"

"You look like someone coated you in honey, and dragged you through a second-hand store," she chided.

"Well then, you won't want to hang around, will you?" I snapped, at once regretful of my uncharacteristically caustic and uncalculated response.

"Aw, don't be like that. What's been eatin' you?" she wanted to know.

"Well, maybe I'm just trying to avoid contact with shitty Mick," I blurted.

"Who's shitty Mick?" she pressed.

"I have absolutely no idea," I admitted. "I reached into the dark and pulled out shitty Mick. I guess I was plumping for some form of deus ex machina."

"Mikie, what the fuck are you talking about?"

"I dunno. I haven't been feeling myself lately."

"So who *have* you been feeling?" she asked. "When you could've been feeling this?"

In accompaniment to her lasciviously brazen rhetoric, she shimmied within the voluminous confines of her quilted purple coat, shooting a skyward glance, and pouting seductively. Despite all my putrescence and hopeless confusion, her playful demeanour and infuriatingly seductive, piercing eyes held me in a quandary, as for a time I considered how it might be to rake my cracked and black-rimmed nails over the pure, pearlescent milk of her soft flesh.

Open-mouthed, I lost myself in her eyes, the playfully fierce hazel rings at once dark and dazzling and flecked with gold. Were it not for my loathsome predicament, we'd soon be tangled in knots of gluttonous lust and exquisitely passionate frustrations.

"As attractive a proposition as that is, I'm gonna need to pass it up," I heard myself whine. "I'm in no condition, neither physically nor mentally."

Crestfallen, she looked to the wilting hogweed at her feet. "Can I use your toilet?" she mumbled.

My devious traitor's heart lurched again at the potential pitfalls of granting Lacey access to my den of sin and debauchery, especially such as it had recently fallen to prognostic squalor and mildew.

"Of course," I relented, stepping back and thus creating a breach of my carefully maintained box of obscene and deplorable secrets.

"Oh, Mikie," she exclaimed, brushing by my shambolic physique. "You stink!"

The words she so eloquently spoke were true. In both character and somatic presentation, I stank. As she went about her necessary ablutions, my malodour threading its spoor into the delicate weft of her fabrics and the tiny, curled hairs of her nostrils, I imagined her reflexive labours as if through an observation hole bored into the bathroom ceiling. Reflected in the lewd and sordid facets of my mind's eye, the crooked trail of her parted hair bobbed as she mopped and dabbed at her luxuriant, accommodating fold.

Immaculate and teasing, the lures of the flesh.

Spangled over the white porcelain of my lavatory.

A fat wasp waylaid in my haphazard web of treachery.

An ambrosial sweet treat of destructive and irreversible poison.

No more, no less than I deserve.

By and by, the commotion of Lacey Beenshill's imminent approach woke me from my largely lustful daydreaming, and I was forced to sustain my rejection of her company in coitus. Manning the open front door like a dismissive sentinel, she again passed me, flashing an expression that I rashly interpreted as pity.

"That's twice you've burned me," she muttered, stepping into the garden.

"Another time, maybe," I lied, knowing full well that my clock was ticking its final tocks, and wouldn't abide another dismally torturous winding.

Nodding dejectedly, she turned and began bouncing her fruitless return journey along my overgrown driveway, leaving me with the ghost of her perfume and my brain wrestling the desire to surge the bathroom in the hope of uncovering sufficient trace of lipid residue to recall our carnal times together. At this, a spirited reprimand from what would now resemble a gigantic, bloated currant, stinking in my kitchen drawer and quelling my every inspiration, however superficially rewarding.

"*If ever Scott takes ill*," the ghastly kidney spake.

I knew it was true. However many years I eluded reprimand, always would the metaphorical cancer of Scott's single kidney blemish my every movement and each waking joy. Forever would the presence of potential penalty and shame shackle me and drive me to my knees in the dirt.

So finally did the dense craters of shadow overwhelm me. Even in the days following the traitor organ's expedience into the great grey void of the sea, I was snared within a vortex of self-deprecation, spiralling uselessly and inexorably down to an even darker fate. I was pitifully afraid of everything, but the lesser of several evils was the reluctant acknowledgement that my life had been ill-spent, and an utter misuse of an opulent set of gleaming tools.

Without ceremony or apology, I eventually hobbled my horribly withered meat to the first floor, to where the brand of Scott's dead cells marked my scullery drawer unclean. From there I clumb to where the ocean subtly salted my curtain and delivered myself unto the earth that it may gorge of my weak blood. Scarce were the imagined niceties of movies and the glamours of a hero's death, as spears of coarse stone punched channels of agony through my ribs. Awash with crimson brine and splintered bone, my heart fought on for an astonishingly long time, allowing me to listen as I choked and gurgled on an unpleasant concoction of seemingly infinite organic swill. Though my eyes stang rebelliously at the lash of saltwater, I was free.

Aces

(Soldiers in the Fields)

Effecting a palpable sense of foreboding and coiled menace, the morning sun teased ticks and groans from the dimly lit corridors of the residential building in which Brent Eurydice and his former friend, slippery, slimy Samuel Sidney the creep had been commissioned to undertake minor repairs on behalf of the company owned by Willie Moon-Stakis. Glorious beams of sunlight criss-crossed the hall like divine lances, filled with reflective rainbow particles of dancing dust. A most warm and enchanting vista, were it not for the questionable dialect of our encroaching labourers, and the damnable carnage their coincidental presence would facilitate forthwith.

Moon-Stakis, skinhead terror of the 1980's synth-pop era, and now odious, eagle-faced building contractor and effortlessly shady motherfucker, had imparted instructions to replace some aged shelving in apartment number 743. Samuel and Brent were somewhat elated at this chickenfeed assignment, having been more accustomed to handballing great articulated lorries stuffed with drywall in predominantly unsavoury locations, such as one polluted corner of the United Kingdom where once a monkey had suffered the gallows on suspicion of being a hostile spy.

Therefore it was with optimism and enthusiasm that the imperfect partnership approached the day's toil, and despite their underlying personal grievances, began to narrow the search for the elusive apartment number 743.

"What's the deal with this bogus fucking key that Willie gave us, anyway?" asked Brent.

"Beats me," said Samuel. "It's not like any key I ever saw."

"It's all academic anyhow," Brent added. "If we can't find the fucking jip-joint."

"Stop being so defeatist," said Samuel. "It ain't the destination, it's all about the *journey*."

"Jesus, who died and made you ghetto guru?"

"You know, you could learn a lot if you'd just open your mind," said Samuel, sarcastically. "Become more of a sentient being. For a young man, you're such a closed book."

"Aw, fuck you," Brent responded.

Throughout the dawn maze they wound and twisted in agitated loops, having scant success in locating the ailing apartment. Despite their combined intelligence they were unable to identify a pattern with which to trace the address that Willie had provided, until salvation appeared in the form of an unusually pretty girl. She was strikingly provocative; dressed in a low-cut top and short pleated skirt, the girl's hourglass hips rocked them like a hurricane as she casually approached the two forlorn figures. Eyeing them curiously over secretarially appropriate eyeglasses, the young men were at once at loggerheads for her attentions and potential affections. With elegance, graces and sleeves filled with aces, she'd pluck at the strings that make boys do fond things.

"Who you lookin' for?" she purred.

"Ain't lookin' for *anybody* any more, sweetheart," slippery, slimy Samuel interjected.

Brent sighed despairingly, rolling his eyes. "Do you live here?" he asked the girl.

"Maybe. What are you, workmen or something?" she asked.

"Yeah," Samuel answered. "Hey, wouldn't it be great if it was your apartment we were gonna be fixing up?"

"Oh, yeah? And why is that?" she challenged.

"Because you could show us where it is, for one thing," Brent interrupted.

"What's the number?"

"My *telephone* number?" asked Samuel.

"Would you shut the fuck up?" Brent scolded.

"Apologies, party-boy," Samuel sneered. "Go ahead, I think she likes you."

"It's seven four three," said Brent, blushing.

"Oh, yeah," said the girl. "I know the one. The apartment numbers are placed according to an algorithm."

"I was just thinking that when you came along," said Brent. "Didn't I say that, Sam? An algorithm?"

"That's right," Samuel goaded. "They covered algorithms in your remedial mathematics class."

Swallowing with difficulty, Brent grappled with a long-standing resentment that swarmed and seethed in response to the caustic remarks. In the interests of the completion of this menial chore, and therefore dodging the ire of Willie Moon-Stakis, he tamped down the steaming, bubbling fury that Samuel had evoked, lest it consume him. The obvious delight of these petty torments and frequently deliberate provocations was smeared across Samuel's smug, slimy chops as he feigned sudden interest in an old newspaper.

"How very remiss of me," Brent hissed.

"This way, guys," the girl clucked from between pink cupid lips, her face framed by long, silky cords of luxuriant black hair.

Snatching up their toolkits and provisions, the barely tolerant twosome scuttled in pursuit of their new, enigmatic benefactor and her flawless American thighs. To their chagrin, apartment number 743 was but a stone's throw away, a premature close to the cabaret.

"Jackpot," Brent exclaimed, dusting his fingers lightly over the door's garish gold font.

"You're welcome," the girl offered.

"Hey, thanks," said Brent. "Although there's one more thing you could help us with, maybe?"

"It's no good, man. She'll never find your dick," Samuel jeered.

Sidestepping Samuel's noted derision, Brent produced the key that Moon-Stakis had provided earlier that morning. A bizarre, bladed curl, it was more akin to a warped medieval bodkin than a device for solving locks and rumbling tumblers.

"What exactly do we do with this?" he asked.

"I'll show you," she cooed, gently sliding the key from between Brent's trembling fingers.

In their proximity, Brent relished the almost ethereal puff of her sweet breath on his chin and lips, and though his eyes were drawn to her delicious, sultry face, despite his efforts to the contrary, they fell upon the stark delineation of her milk-white titties. Consequently averting his gaze, he returned his attention to the task at hand.

"Sorry," he whispered, knowing full well he'd been compromised.

"I don't know if it matters," she replied curiously.

Certain that Samuel would be positively exploding with lurid responses to their brief and subtle exchange, Brent observed fixedly as the girl set about engaging some curious, hidden mechanism with the twisted tip of the key. Presently, the door opened with nary a creak or a worrisome din, reflections of serenity and quietude within.

"You *dog*," Samuel commended, although it was unclear to whom he alluded.

"Thanks again," Samuel fawned. "We'd have been here all day if it wasn't for you."

What happened next occurred so quickly and abruptly, and with such fleet ferocity that Brent would have measured difficulty recounting the incident in the following days. As Samuel sidled into apartment 743, scooping a potentially chronic *blunt* from a deep pocket of his sagging Moon-Stakis overalls, the formerly placid starlet launched herself upon his person and proceeded to gnash through his fabrics, goring deep and sanguinary wounds into his leg.

"What the shit is this?!" Brent howled, staring in stark disbelief as she continued the assault.

Blood splashed the polished wooden floor as the felled Samuel screamed in agony, his hands beating wildly at the girl to little avail. In his abject horror, Brent regarded her feral face and the sudden manifestation of raging hostility therein. Where moments ago, her eyes had been pure pearls of youthful clarity and curiosity, they were now red, veined balls of primal aggression in a blue-hued face abound with lesions and peppered with an unpleasant blend of blood, gristle and slaver. Rudely robbed of any opportunities to further woo the young lady with the hips against which all women should grade themselves, Brent registered a faint sting as his previously wounded heart sustained further injury. At this, it was time to make a desperate stand, and to attempt to rescue his wailing, flailing, blood-frothed former friend from the jaws of the opportunistic succubus. Regardless of his associate's hereditary leanings toward being a fat, sweaty dick, complications would be considerably compounded upon having to explain why he observed Samuel being bitten to within an inch of his pathetic destination before responding in an amicable manner.

Projecting that within their respective tool bags there'd be an item befitting the task of bludgeoning single white females driven by a supernatural appetite for living human flesh, Brent clawed at the hardy fabric of the nearest kit, throwing wide its self-adhering seam with a satisfying tearing noise. Therein lay a most surprising object; gleaming under the glare of the morning sun, resplendent in its lethal potential, was a lovingly maintained sawed-off shotgun, the mere possession of which carried a minimum penalty of five years in the pokey (or the *stony lonesome*, if you will). Legislation aside, it seemed that Willie Moon-Stakis, affable in his dangerously casual indifference, had laid on an overwhelmingly pertinent Easter egg.

Cradling the weight of the weapon in his hands, Brent was markedly comforted, although he continued to shake like a chihuahua negotiating a troublesome stool under unnecessary environmental duress. Galvanised by the cries of his fallen colleague, he reluctantly swung the weapon to bear on the wild girl's dome and thumbed its twin hammers, assuming it to be loaded.

A cataclysmic wall of sound assailed the two men as the highly collectible weapon discharged a burst of fire and wickedly murderous steel bearings. Where once the girl's sweet head had rested upon creamy shoulders as smooth as porcelain, it now blew apart in a voluminous cloud of rapidly dispersing blood and brain, hair and bone. When the buckshot hit, she done got her wig split. In the interests of personal safety, Brent had peeled her cap back.

In wake of the carnage, in accompaniment to the ringing in his ears, Samuel's persistent sniffles and whimpering brought Brent's attention to their most urgent predicament. Considering the crimson walls slithering with warm gobs of the young lady's dying cells, her undeniably sexy corpse leaking blood and piss onto the rustic oak floor, and slippery Samuel's potentially fatal wound, what could possibly go wrong?

"Help me, Brent," Samuel pleaded, clutching pathetically at his gnawed and bloody thigh.

"What would you like me to do?" Brent queried calmly. "I neutralized the threat, didn't I?"

"You've gotta help me, man," he persisted. "You saw her face, her fuckin' loony red eyes! What if I turn like her? You dunno what was wrong with her."

In a maelstrom of whirling emotions and cold panic, Brent's coherence floated in a pinprick of light, on a life-preserving hoop of soothing ignorance and suspiciously linear clarity.

"This isn't the movies, Sam. Although it seems you're at a rather grievous disadvantage."

"Don't fuck about with me, mate. I can feel that shit inside me, cloning me and whatnot."

"Sam, you're hysterical."

"Jesus, so would you be," Samuel whined. "Some voodoo fuckin' calendar model starts going postal on my leg, and now her brains are drying on my face! Her fuckin' hair's in my mouth, man!"

"Wrap your fucking belt around your leg," Brent suggested.

"A little help, man," Samuel pleaded. "I'm fucking bleeding to death, you streak of shit!"

Breathing deeply, Brent attempted to regulate his wildly racing heart and quivering hands.

"Well, it's like this, Sam," Brent began. "It's been a frightfully long time since we saw eye to eye, if we ever did. This unholy shit-show has kinda put things in perspective. You could say I've undergone something of an epiphany."

"I'm fucking dying, man," Samuel sobbed, speckled with gore. "This isn't the road to Damascus, you muggy cunt!"

"We're in this up to our necks anyway," said Brent, coldly. "There's no way back from this fucking disaster. So, it occurs to me that in all the long years we've been friends, in every catastrophe that ever transpired since I was a kid, there's always been one reliable common factor."

"Yeah, and what's that?"

"You," said Brent. "You've always been at the heart of every major disruption in my life since I could cross the road unsupervised."

"Please, man. This isn't the time."

"No fault of your own, I guess," Brent went on. "We were always trying to outdo each other. Always jealous when the other one got somethin' sweet. So, I'm faced with a decision. How much do I want to erase the fucking blight on my life that you've become?"

"Shoot my leg off, man," Samuel implored. "Please. It's like she had worms or some shit on her teeth, and I can feel them crawling inside me. Please, mate."

"Worms are the least of our problems, Sam. What are folk gonna think if they find me with an illegal firearm, a dead girl with no head and an incoherent, blithering fool with one leg?"

"I'll testify, man," Samuel murmured. "Please, gimme a break. I'm cold, Brent. I'm shivering."

"Oddly enough, I don't feel a hundred percent, myself," said Brent. "But I reckon I'll keep it together until I see what happens to you."

Quaking, ghastly white and breathing in ragged, shallow gasps, slippery, slimy Samuel was gradually bleeding out from a hole in his leg, the approximate size that it could comfortably accommodate thirty years of being cheated. If the spreading pool of blood in which he languished were to be any indication, he hadn't long to try and take it back.

"You're quiet for once in your life, Sam," said Brent. "Are you feeling any bloodthirsty, otherworldly compulsions, or are you just gonna shut that overloaded, fat heart down and get the fuck out of my story?"

Wheezing softly, Samuel maintained his silence, although the glistening orbs of his eyes remained coherent and were bruised cerise. In the absence of police sirens or any such meddlesome anxieties, Brent arranged himself comfortably to wait the shit out.

The Urban Legend of Geordie-Pop
(Eulogy for Holy Field)

Act One

An English waiting room in a doctor's surgery; 1974, the year of Zaire's rumble. Predominant shades of orange, brown and natural wood throughout. Flattened cigarette stubs litter the floor and accumulate within the great glass ashtrays that have colourful pills and inoculating sharps securely inlaid, to the constant wonderment of a never-ending succession of anxious children. Curling, yellowing posters adorn the walls, hopelessly discouraging the use of motorcars whilst under the influence of alcohol and emphasising the demerit of excessive physical force when discharging discipline among minors. One such public service announcement featured a young boy, his face bloody and slick with tears, serving mainly as a parental aid as mothers commonly warned their charges that those wounds were the unseemly results of nose-picking. All this, while the lizard-king crooned some pure, white-hot rock and roll moods from the wireless radio behind the glass-fronted reception desk. Hardly an idyllic scene, but it was honest. It was the 1970's.

Nothing unusual about this medical amenity, save for one distinguishing factor that set it apart from anywhere else in the world. Bold as brass, a black cat sassed, fussed and mussed by grubby little hands abound with microscopic germs. Such was the effectiveness of the cat's calming nature upon the children of this small quarter that staff and patients had long opted to turn a blind eye to protocol. Geordie-Pop, as the black tomcat was fondly dubbed, had been appeasing distressed infants in the doctor's waiting room for longer than anyone would have deemed naturally possible. No sooner would a sobbing child step in from the cold, fearful of pokes, prods, infections and injections, than Geordie-Pop would materialise and apply his effective brand of softly administered head-butts, purrs and licks. Never stinky, Geordie-Pop stolidly prepared his flock for the examination rooms so successfully that he was considered an asset as opposed to a tolerance, and lesser felines in the vicinity were regularly mistaken for his grace.

As all good things must come to an end (so the adage goes); Geordie-Pop's surgery was eventually razed to the ground and relocated as part of a new multifunctional community hospital, the modern, stringent regulations of which would not be manipulated to accommodate the blagging of favour from domestic animals. In light of this development, Geordie-Pop was never seen again and subsequently elevated to legendary status, his tale passed through the generations and frequently embellished to include such preposterous notions as basic speech and the capability of flight.

Act Two

Bobbing, floating freely along like being born.

The easy bounce and the freedom of the night city.

Contentedly exhausted, Trotter Long ran the final furlong to his home, his lungs feeling clean and refreshed; inner harmony restored, legs capable and supple. For him, running the streets of his home town in selective sportswear was as essential as the breaking of daily bread.

The wide, circular cul-de-sac of Letsby Avenue was welcomingly lit by the amber glow of the streetlights. Around the neatly manicured lawns, bronzed leaves nestled at the fast approach of autumn; yet the air was warm, carrying the scent of blossom and a hint of the freshly laundered, nurturing characteristics of each saintly house. You'd be forgiven for suspecting the widespread application of layers of sickly, sycophantic fakery as lichen-coated concrete cherubs spouted water into lily-padded pools, their protection assured by the token addition of lacquered picket fencing and a cursory neighbourhood watch scheme. Moths surrounded the varying arrangements of porch lamps and solar garden lights, casting softly dancing shadows over synthetic cobbled driveways (for those averse to the higher maintenance synonymous with the soothing crunch of tires on coarse shingle). Aside from the jungle rules of high school, this suburban utopia was all young Trotter had known. All the neighbourhood mothers baked fairy cakes with sparkling silver sprinkles, all the families held yard sales with home-made iced lemonade, and gnomes sat contentedly fishing from toadstool seats among their edelweiss. A grand guignol of smoke and mirrors intended to hinder the horrifying biological truth that every kid in the street learning to ride their shiny new bicycle was present because Daddy ploughed Mama's bean field and she liked it. Behind the facade of exclusive knitting circles and goofy golf trousers, nobody's clinically bleached anus yielded roses.

Popping out his electronic earphones, Trotter basked in the aura of middle-class splendour, the stillness marred only by the acidic hiss of dated rock and roll from his bluetooth accessory. Slick with perspiration, he relished the notion of a toxic catharsis due to his recent physical exertions. Even the blistering of his feet held a clean nobility from which he derived an aspect of pride. Snagging the keys from his pocket, he approached his house and the easy convenience of its consistent luxuries, such as a hot shower to blast away his stink and the subsequent balm of the jets of pressurised water on his ailing muscles. Following his ablutions, his cool, clean and fluffy bed would be ready to float him off to a safe night-time adventure during which his academic batteries would recharge in time for morning, and another potentially lucrative scholastic campaign.

Unbeknownst to Trotter, as he crossed the spotless threshold into number 23, he was about to participate in a scarcely believable tale of terror spanning great intervals of space and time that would change his life completely, and without any possibility of amendment.

"Hi, son," said his father with an almost *sitcom* enthusiasm. "How was your run?"

"Not bad, Daddy-o," he replied. "Can't wait to hit the showers, but."

"You go get 'em, sport," said Dad. "Why, when I was your age, it was like my running shoes had rockets tied to 'em."

"Not so fast nowadays, Dad," Trotter joked, marginally unsettled by his father's uncharacteristic exuberance.

"Hey, you keep up that lip, you'll see I can still lick ya."

"Sure thing, Dad," said Trotter, mounting the staircase. "Is Ma' home?"

"You betcha," said Father. "Right there in the kitchen gett'n busy with some finger-lickin' chicken platter. Smells great, doesn't it?"

"Sure does, Pop," said Trotter; and it did.

"You get your stanky ass upstairs and hit the shower, then maybe you can rifle through the leftovers," announced his father with a wink.

"I'm on it," Trotter replied.

"Get outta town," said Father, the hall light reflected on his pink, barren dome.

Feeling as if he'd unwittingly embarked on a sugar-coated episode of some old show that was loaded with thinly veiled Christian morality and idealistic guidelines to the perfect existence, Trotter clumb the stairs and began shedding his soiled clothes, simultaneously shrugging off notions of unease. Although his father had played an attentive role in his upbringing, it wasn't always standard practice to greet him in the porch with such enthusiasm towards his fitness regime, nor was it commonplace for his mother to prepare a batch of fried chicken. Despite the facade presented by their freshly waxed car and weathervane incorporating a gilded cock, their weekday meals generally consisted of heavily processed convenience crap from boxes in the freezer, combined with a medically adequate pseudo-potato compound. Nevertheless, in the hand-over-fist cast of modern teenagers in the grip of an overprivileged social delusion, he'd take the damn fried chicken.

Presently, the freshly aromatic and suitably hygienic Trotter Long entered the kitchen of number 23, swathed in his thick and shockingly flammable dressing-gown, immediately detecting that the situation was awry. His mother, more accustomed to the errant splashing of ketchup and warm grease onto her pristine clothes (accompanied by a flare of baffled and indignant expletives), was decked out in an apron emblazoned with cupcakes. His father sat mincingly cross-legged, nursing a gently smouldering pipe in his shirtsleeves and browsing a dog-eared newspaper. Such a charming domestic scene was unknown beyond the synthetic veneer of the Christmas holidays, and unless Trotter was about to be blindsided with a jolting injection of bad news, then strange things were most certainly afoot.

"Here's our handsome boy," Father announced from below his ebullient moustache.

"Hi, sweetie," said Mother, smiling widely. "I sure hope you're hungry."

"What's all this?" asked Trotter, bemused.

"What's wrong, honey?" Mother enquired, crestfallen. "Don't you *love* fried chicken any more?"

"Yeah, I do. But what's the occasion? We usually have waffles, or spaghetti sauce from a carton."

"Waffles ain't gonna turn those shoulders into boulders, boy," his father answered.

"Would you rather I made spaghetti, honey?" Mother appealed. "It's no trouble at all."

"No, chicken's good," said Trotter, cautiously eyeing the mound of steaming, battered chicken drumsticks dominating the kitchen table. "It's just a little unusual for you to go to all this trouble. And since when did you smoke a pipe, Dad? I only ever saw guys smoking pipes in old movies."

"Maybe you just took your eye off the ball, son," Father suggested. "If you ain't fast, you're last."

His trepidation peaking, Trotter reluctantly seated himself within dashing distance of the hall, suddenly deeply suspicious of his birth parents and their peculiarly uncommon behaviour. Such were his misgivings that he was wholly expectant of a filtered barrage of canned laughter to accompany his father's next corny quip, and the announcement that this episode of *Letsby Avenue* was recorded in front of a live studio audience.

"Anyway, thanks, Ma'," he murmured, reaching hungrily for a hunk of hot hen.

"Woah there, hotshot," his father admonished. "Stay cool, junior. We ain't said grace."

"Oh, what kind of horse-shit is this?" Trotter warbled, standing. "This isn't a Sunday-school picnic, and it ain't a TV show! What's going on, and why are you acting like this?"

"Well, we were hoping to resolve this amicably, or at least covertly," said Father.

"What?" Trotter yelled. "What's wrong?"

As Trotter stood in hopeful expectation of a relatively orthodox explanation to the evening's eccentricities, his assumed father solemnly beheld him, his eyes rolling back in their sockets to reveal flawless orbs of white, yet the boy was in no doubt of their continued function. Shimmering and pearlescent, they betrayed nothing, while beneath them flicked a slithering black tongue, glistening wet like a great, fat leech.

"Ma'?" Trotter beseeched of his mother, her voluminous auburn wig blurred beyond his tears of panic and bewilderment.

Her jolly depictions of cupcake euphoria were suddenly a blatantly unpalatable mockery of his emotional distress, and like the imposter that wore his father's characteristics, her eyes yielded to both the chilling spheres of a most predatory stripe, and the tell-tale tongue of an insidious and covetous hunter.

Snatching a drumstick from the ellipsoid serving platter and flinching by nature of its residual heat, Trotter broke the crisp, crumbling nugget in twain, wholly expectant of a legion of writhing maggots or perhaps a telltale quantity of powdered sedative. Instead, for a very short time, his efforts were rewarded by a spark; a fleeting green vector, its loops and whorls describing the variations and fluctuations in density within the meat's phantom fabrication. The aroma from the breached dough was a special scent of ashes and electrical discharge, reminiscent of the piquancy surrounding a cranial blunt force trauma. In a reflexive spasm of heightened agitations, Trotter dropped the malevolent fried chicken, lest its malignancy curdle his blood and pollute his purity, such as his kin had been evidently soured.

"What's with the fucking laser-food?" he screamed.

Silently, the father-lizard advanced on Trotter's position, dismissively nonchalant following the compromise of their outrageous duplicity. Faced with no immediately apparent option but to physically defend himself, Trotter grabbed at the creature's arms, fending off its presumably unwholesome intentions, and was astonished at its fallacious lack of substance. In the grip of mortal combat, the father-lizard's limbs, while strong, were no more abundant than the whirling of an empty tracksuit, or the manual management of a dimensionally comparable dirigible. A struggle ensued, such as is generally ascertained at a crime scene via the discovery of toppled chairs and a host of scuffs and suspicious abrasions. During the altercation, in consequence of the reptile's absence of recognisable density, Trotter was able to crudely stuff his former father's soft body through the kitchen window and out onto the lawn, where more of their kind had accumulated in silent assembly. Faced with a terrifying choice of fight or flight, he projected no positive denouement to grappling with the lizard-mother currently eyeing him balefully, and bolted from the scullery in anticipation of the hopeful freedom of Letsby Avenue. Hang the consequences of pounding the tar happed in a gown and slippers; circumstances dictated that emergency contingencies were now in full and severe effect, and he took to the streets with a hunger borne of the animal instinct to survive.

Outwardly deserted, the estate and its normalities seemed to goad his predicament. The miniature woodcutter continued to chop at his eternally plentiful stock, spinning in the breeze atop the pocked tree stump at the foot of the Long's Garden, and the night-slugs attacked the scraps of mould-speckled bread thrown out for the birds.

High in the sky, the moon shone proud and bright, a useless white delight for a young man in flight tonight. Alone and half-grown, yet blessed of strong and stout bone, Trotter Long ran for the rainy hills and the forfeit of hewn wood and stone, and somewhere to call his own.

Keen to be absorbed within the serenity and rural integrity of the nearby greenbelt, he made for the unkempt path running parallel to the battered and robbed-out railway line once heavy with coal-conveying traffic. Here, he was importuned by a wailing young girl, presumably dispatched by the same colony of usurpers that had waylaid his parents. Close at his heels, her grotesquely elongated mouth issued an unearthly and discouraging clamour, such that would serve a multiple purpose. The maudlin cries of an infant amid the tranquillity of wasteland would serve to alarm the public and invariably incriminate the fleeing boy, thus stymieing his abdication; and in addition to inspiring terror within Trotter's already damaged psyche, the girl's repulsive caterwauling would also alert affiliated parties as to her current location. Her arms, unnaturally long and flexible, were extended in pincer fashion, mocking his abject fear and intimidation as her yellow cardigan draped, sodden with rain.

Trotter's disadvantage appeared overwhelming, as at any moment he expected to be compromised by more of the rudely reptilian invaders and subjected to whatever conversion process they advocated, or the liquefaction and consumption of his mortal mass and subsequent mimicry of his most personal idiosyncrasies. Thistles and brambles whipped and tore at his bare ankles, sapping his resolve as blood and dew dappled his skin. Slowing inexorably, he prepared to submit to fate and whatever injuries of earth may facilitate it.

Then, as all hope diminished and drained from his perception like day destroys the night, there came a sound as of the rushing and pushing of a natural entity of fearsome proportions.

Sticks and twigs all snapped and crackled, sod dislodged, and stones were rattled; the drumming thunder of beastly paw and building skirl from feline maw.

With a ferocity tenfold that of its compact build, a great cat burst from the hedgerow with hell in its eyes and a kink in its tail-tip. Amid this holy field, the sooty, heroic cloud of whirling claws and trap-like incisors smote the cardiganed fiend, driving its flimsy body into the deep and unforgiving snags of the undergrowth before disappearing as suddenly as it had lent its grace and altruism. Quite unaware of the significance of the rare and mythical honour from which he'd prevailed, Trotter Long ran on, capitalising on the opportunity to make good his escape; to what ends, nobody knew.

As for the cat, contentedly chewing his claws in some unknown capacity with an air of domesticated feline arrogance and self-satisfaction, it seemed that even in this troubled age, Geordie-Pop was still tending his flock. Though with each generation the memory diminished, his love endured, in one form or another.

The Oldest Soak

(What's the Score with Teas, Dale?)

Jock Ross, lush of the valley, benevolent barfly and enigma of the three points meandered along the breadth of the stubborn old marina, dangerously free. This aged dockland was a sweet, sour and solid throwback to an age of iron, steam and coal, and largely overlooked by recent generations of *pings* and things. If one could disregard the sprigs of green grass sprouting from blocked gutters and fissures in the cast iron drainpipes along the way, the succulent clumps of emerald moss ensconced in the disused tram lines and the fluorescent orange of the life preservers, it was possible (with some pure imagination) to regress to a time when lives were immortalised within the grey and sepia tones of monochrome photography. The stout and sodden wood piles of the wharf were silent witness to a depth of avoidable tragedy and scores of harsh, forgotten seasons since the broad animal mothers who drove them had lain in the earth. As their clandestine roots are eaten away to become soft and oily weed, so are all secrets eventual; their integrity dying foremost, and hardest.

Largely oblivious to his mixed heritage, Jock Ross ambled on, lager sloshing around his tiny gut. Once a thriving residential quarter, only a few houses remained along the harbour front; tall and thin, gaunt and harrowed. Surrounded by grassy wasteland, sullied by cold and sucking swamps of eternal slurry, the bleak houses were yet equipped with inlaid boot scrapers, their cavities padded with sun-faded crisp packets half-filled with rainwater and settled sediment; a world within a world. Since the squandering of his leisure time weighed little upon the anxieties of the slight and spry Ross, he considered the simpler folk who'd once populated this derelict suburb, and subsequently noticed that the green door to star-crossed number 3 was temptingly ajar.

Cheekily curious by nature, and further bolstered by the warm beer in his belly, Jock approached the worn, sagging and algae-coated doorstep, and with a furtive glance in all directions, ascertained his solitary standing and gingerly prodded the door amid blistered shamrock paint. Presenting minimal resistance it opened with a juddering, giggling creak, granting passage to a rare slice of authentic retrospective preservation. His initial observation was that of smell; the subtle odour of boiled egg and a hint of brown bread, a regretful transgression of a lady, now dead. Leaning further through the veil of history, justifiably fearful of reprisal against his trespass, his eyes fed greedily of a wonderfully sweet conglomerate of clover green and ivory cream decor. *Green and cream, cream and green; a rustic, rural, butter churn dream.* Flushed with a mixture of animal curiosity and the euphoric rush of uncharacteristic criminal pursuit, Jock made his way into the grotty hall.

Lulled by the authentic butterfly kisses of damp spotting the textured ivory wallpaper throughout, he cared not a whit for its damaging potential; enchanted, was he, by the quaint and personal furnishings assailed by aged and knotted cobwebs and lashings of peppery dust. Jock was, by now, unmindful of compromise, and reached out to investigate a set of drawers, neat, petite and set upon legs turned to a squat and satisfying arrangement of scoops and bulges. With a hollow, whistling scrape, the lower drawer slid open to reveal a boxed cassette tape of some note, itself a casualty of the pervading dampness and extreme temperatures permitted by the poorly seal of the front door. Red lettering on the case denoted it was some form of popular video game, and though the character depicted was of a cheerfully optimistic stamp, his cobalt-blue surroundings were tainted and pocked with mildew, creating a self-contained juxtaposition. Though the cassette was of marked interest, Jock was currently ambitious for the discovery of greater, tastier tuck, and made for the sisal staircase, its risers battered and chipped, its apex mysteriously ominous and forbidding.

Above him, a slash of unfettered daylight glared with hostility from the landing, loaded with imagined acrophobic mockery and unknown menace; the period of trepidation before the mouse clambers aboard the killing floor to snatch of the cheese and is cleft in twain, its spine bent double, and innards pulped through the breached anus by means of unmerciful triggered steel. Jock clumb regardless, compelled by an unrelenting compulsion, a curiosity of fabled proportions a whisper shy of the label *destiny*. On unfamiliar terrain, each step that took him closer to the bounty of the landing was an unconscious imitation of childhood treachery; the shifting of weight twixt load-bearing leg and pivotal grip upon thickly painted banister in pursuit of illicit *big bickies*. Mounting the final riser, he relaxed to some note, lest he betray his stealth with the honking creak of a dilapidated floorboard, its iron teeth squalling upon being wrest from snug and moist embrace.

Jaded and tilted portraits regarded him listlessly from behind a veil of dust and decades, their gaze ineffectual and indistinct. Presenting a single portal, the stair head was a perfect square of scuffed and bobbled carpet beyond which a sliver of untapped curiosities shone tantalisingly through the very narrowest of apertures. Drawn as a moth to its blinkered fate, bumping frenziedly at the tarnished, impenetrable glass of an arc-sodium lure, he peered through the crack with a gleaming, hungry eye. The scene beyond this door was much as the hall had been, although trinkets and baubles were in greater abundance. Within his limited scope was a glimmering fireplace; recessed ivory marble and speckled tiles upon which reclined all manner of antiquated fireside accessories and pinned horse brasses. Such was the gluttony with which his eyes devoured this unprotected haven, that when coupled with his exhilaration at the foolhardy assumption of being its sole benefactor, he overlooked the gently glowing coals of a dying fire, and the subtle, but unmistakable whine of flitting electrons in a CRT television. Lit by the selfish notion of free digs and a caboose in which to cool his heels, reclining with bottles of sweet wine and amber beers, he pressed at the door's cheap manufacture with the intention of creating a breach through which to wriggle his bony hips. At the door's base, a fan of worn and agitated carpet was revealed as it scraped an arc on silent hinges, and as he negotiated the protesting vehicle with his glaikit, bulbous bonce, so it became glaringly apparent that he wasn't alone.

In one corner of the room there stood a remarkably robust wooden tank of a television set supported by thin, but nonetheless adequate cast iron legs and charming castors, on which was displayed a classic boxing contest in gloriously elegant black and white. Resplendent in his ghastly and crackling pallor was a combatant whose designated title shared an aural correspondence to *shimmy riled*; and in addition to the thousands in attendance, watching from the comfort of a time-worn and fashionably outdated armchair, was a furrowed and liver-spotted old man. In the fleeting seconds it took Jock to register that he'd unwittingly trespassed on an occupied property, he failed to assess the senior citizen's current condition. Dead or alive, he figured it wasn't worth the risk of an arrest for public nuisance and noisily fled the scene, concluding that today's capacity for misadventure had been exceeded. Closing the door with exaggerated nonchalance, he left *shimmy riled* and the extraordinary mister mortis to their own devices.

During the next few days, given time to embrace sobriety and reflect upon any niggling nuances over which alcohol may have waved a productive and creative wand, Jock began to wonder if the strange case of mister mortis and his armoured television incorporating authentic medieval construct hadn't been an invention of his ale-soaked sleeping brain. Although in no doubt that he'd ambled home via the old ferry, he felt compelled to question the validity of a memory in which he'd violated an old guy's privacy and unwittingly *bogarted* on his preciously limited recreation time. The addition of the computer cassette tape, horse brass and the fireside brush and shovel were likely delirium's answer to garnish; a cherry on the top, if you will. Under the harsh light of Monday to Friday's workaday schedule, the whole bizarre affair adopted an absurd, surreal flavour; yet the experience seemed to have dug barbed hooks into his frontal lobe, and the cord that secured them kept dragging him back to ponderation of what was now an annoying and persistent quandary.

Dropping a sober house call on the old guy was out of the question. Jock was doubtful that any quantity of liberally applied *smooth talkin' jive* would pacify a chap of his advanced years when affronted with a revelation of trespass and covert observations. It seemed that situations demanded a return to form, and a dubiously spontaneous drunken meandering during which he'd be better equipped to confront his aged acquaintance and offer a more palatable explanation as to why he'd interrupted his big-time super Saturday.

And so it unfolded that Jock Ross found himself avoiding the worrisome glare of headlights along the marina, poised at the stoop of star-crossed number 3 with a bobbing head, a pocketful of small change and a beat-up cigarette packet containing one or two tortured and buckled smokes. Again fortified by the liquor circulating his sinewy form, he was nevertheless surprised to find that in response to a moderate nudge, the green door opened again with the same menacing, gurgling guffaw as before. Despite his misgivings at such an alarmingly unlikely coincidence, he bounced through the portal and out of the long, elastic shadows of the dockland road, intruding on the deeply portentous murk of the mortis' porch.

The house was so much spookier in the darkness of the night, when the gloom was absolute and he's preparing for a fright. When cobwebs brush his fingers and there's guano at his toes, the things beneath the earth will come a-tearing at his clothes.

The plucky Jock ascended, desirous of the sanctuary of faintly flickering light ahead, and despite the pervading shadows he noticed a detail he'd missed on the previous incursion. The increments of an improvised growth chart had been etched onto the gloss paint of the door frame in various colours of ink, recording the progress of ANNIE. Coupled with the rapid strobing of the nearby TV and its accompanying whine, the infantile scrawl of the solitary word effected a sullen undertone. Whatever had become of the wistful Annie, she was most definitely *not* okay.

Abandoning Annie with the same nonchalance as so many others had done, Jock squeezed his blonde melon into the light with another baffled rasp of abraded carpet, enjoying a welcoming warmth that conveyed a mixture of dubious essences. The traditionally downtrodden aroma of chip fat and a long-absent canine were as permanent as woe in this saloon, as was a dogged determination to hold fast to a barely remembered generation. As before, the bespectacled old man reclined before his juggernaut CRT, a misty glass in hand and a disinterested glare on his deeply lined and leathery face. On the screen, an archaic game show played out. If the man had registered an intruder in his midst, he gave less of a fuck than he did about his overflowing ashtray, or the Jennings family who were about to miss out on the chance of winning a speedboat.

"Sorry to bother you, sir," Jock ventured, humbly. "Your front door was open."

"That's right, Jock," said the man, in a strained and reedy voice.

"You know me?" asked Jock, taken aback.

"No," said the man, his East London twang as stark as the ironed crease in his ill-fitting jeans. "Not really."

"How did you know my name, then?" Jock asked.

"I've 'eard of you, round the doors." answered the man.

Deeply puzzled, Jock was nevertheless relieved that the skeletal man wasn't a cadaver as he'd initially suspected, and relaxed to some measure.

"Why do you leave your door unlocked?" Jock wanted to know. "It's dangerous round here."

"Why not?" asked the man, defiantly. "Who's gonna come in 'ere? Most people don't even notice the place. I've got nuffin' that anyone would want, anyway."

Amid the brown, scallop-patterned carpet and unkempt bookshelves, below the tasselled lampshades and textured ceiling, partitioned from the world by heavy crushed velvet curtains and reflected in the glass of a giant whisky bottle holding copper coins, Jock Ross shifted awkwardly, juxtaposed between a desire to flee this satirical farce and a compelling curiosity that centred round his peculiar host. Toes pointed inward, heels apart, he picked at a crescent of dirt beneath his fingernail.

"So why aren't you yelling at me to get out?" Jock asked. "Or shoving a bayonet blade in my face or something?"

"You don't bother me none," said the man. "And I never done any active service."

"No, I just thought, you know. It's an old house, with old things."

"Yeah. Maybe the oldest."

Never shifting his gaze from the television, the old man afforded little to alleviate Jock's discomposure, exhibiting minimal anxiety as a result of his presence. On the thick convex screen, the Jennings family regretfully accepted their consolation prizes.

"You don't mind my being here?" Jock asked.

"Make yourself at 'ome while you still can," the man suggested. "Won't be long before they've pulled this all down to make room for more *nig-nogs* and Chinese takeaways and that."

"You mind if I smoke?" Jock asked, politely playing down the man's old-time racism.

"Are you joking? Smoke 'em while you got 'em," the man answered. "When our number's up, it won't be thanks to cigarettes, I can tell ya that much for nuffin'."

"What do you mean?" asked Jock.

"Well," the man began. "That's a story for another time. Sit yourself down, will ya? You're makin' the place look untidy."

"Thanks," said Jock, *parking his eye* on the edge of the settee's cushion, fearful of what malignant detritus might be snagged twixt its upholstered lips. "So who are you?"

"Ted," he answered, curtly.

"Ted? That's it?"

"Yeah, what d' you want?" Ted demanded. "Sir Ted? Technician Ted? Nah, it's just Ted."

"So what are you watching?" Jock enquired.

"Some old game show," Ted replied. "Load of old crap it is, an' all. I like watchin' the boxing, but it's thin on the ground tonight. Beggars can't be choosers. Stone the crows."

On recognition of the poorly rendered image on the screen, Jock was inclined to agree. The production left a lot to be desired compared to modern standards, although it was a great deal more honest at face value. The Jennings family looked crestfallen following receipt of their runner-up merchandise, yet they were contractually obligated to smile like new parents. The results were Lovecraftian, freakish.

"Whyncha get the drinks in?" Ted suggested, tilting his empty glass. "There's more in the cupboard, there."

"You're sure?" asked Jock. "I can disappear if you like."

"Everyone I know disappears in the end," Ted replied. "Might as well keep me company now you're here."

"I'll take it easy, but," said Jock. "I'm already comfortably in my cups, as they say."

"Yeah, so I see," Ted added. "You're so pissed you probably think JFK is still alive."

"Nice one," Jock chuckled. "I think I'll use that one myself, should the situation arise."

"Knock yourself out, sunshine. I ain't got no claims on it."

As the evening wore on, so the atmosphere gradually warmed and it transpired that both men had acquired a companion of sorts. Despite its felonious preamble, the whole unseemly event could even be recounted as an amicable meeting; numerous topics being openly discussed and controversial opinions cheerfully exchanged. Ted's whisky flowed unreservedly, and having eventually overcome its stabbing bitterness, was appreciated in excess by the newly established Johnson & Ross conglomerate until daylight permeated the thick curtains and the birds commenced their infernal dawn racket. Reluctantly, the woefully inebriated Jock Ross politely excused himself and took to his perilously unsteady heels. Prior to his departure it was suggested they should convene again, under more civilised terms and less of a case of misadventure spliced with unlawful entry. Upon acceptance the summit was adjourned, and a new confidante had been unknowingly selected.

"You can take that cassette you were lookin' at earlier, if you want it?" Ted offered.

"Oh, yeah," said Jock. "I don't have the hardware to run it anymore, but it's a nice bit of nostalgia."

"Ain't no use to me," said Ted. "It belonged to my granddaughter, see."

Jock snagged the game cassette from the quaint set of drawers and bade his new friend farewell, tactfully spurning the fresh can of worms that Ted had offered, lest the fate of the evanescent Annie become the subject of further protracted exchange. Despite being incorrigibly intrigued, its mystery would withstand another day of absent daydreaming and projection, whereas it was debatable whether Jock's liquor-riddled carcass could endure more than another few minutes of sleep deprivation before triggering mandatory shutdown.

Off he marched into the rising sun and aspirations of deep, rejuvenating sleep, little dreaming of the merciless, inexorable black hole into which he was being drawn at the hands of the hapless, dithering old sot that was Ted Johnson. Clutching the rattling and mildewed video game, stumbling, fumbling and absently mumbling, he wound his weary way away from the menacing, biding river and its potential as a darkly lethal tributary in a series of heinous events. Oblivious to his own fetid, grasping fate, his shoes scraped and bumped of the flagstones' shelly compound, the morning sunlight dazzling his eyes and further shrouding his woolly view. The obtrusive litter of the streets that he trod and booted could one day be swept along and swallowed in an all-consuming, destructive throat of cold water, along with those of its manufacture.

Blessed ignorance; folly of the young and the protector of innocence until such a time as we are considered hardy enough to endure its arrows and calloused knuckles, healing its gores and divots. Then, with blind faith and hope shall we charge into a fray of broken hearts and the inevitable pockets of bone-splitting grief that will temper our constitutions or dissolve our will until stooped and weeping shadows are all that remain for us to shuffle among the living. We are but a seemingly inexhaustible supply of expendable, commerce-generating living meat, the likes of which typically engender less consideration than a fluttering flake of tawny shit in singular form.

That said, the wearisome Jock finally collapsed into his cot, dropping his newly acquired video game to the floor where the clamshell case broke open, its tangled and corrupted magnetic tape springing free like aggressively stubborn and dense pubes.

Spring ran its customary course; bobbing yellow trumpet-heads, clouds of aggressive flying annoyance and plenty of sunshine interspersed with the lightest of rainbow rains. People sneezed as buds and bulbs split asunder, and the old gods seemed appeased as new life bloomed voraciously, even from death. Below warm and fluffy speedwell skies, fireplaces and thick coats were deserted in favour of parks and beaches where sharp, hardy grasses were trampled, broken and daubed with blobs of errant ice cream and guaranteed tears. The great, golden, sweating disco disc in the sky charged the gluttonous hemisphere with its life-generating rays of blinding light, encouraging fun for all, and eventually sighing into the *gastro-funnel* turbo boost of summer. Cascades of coins of all persuasions, trinkets, penknives and cracked plastic cups, hot soup for Grandma, plastic flasks emblazoned with space-saga heroes and toffee wrappers filled with spit; cardboard box villages, seaside sandwiches and hillbillies with malfunctioning water-rifles, hot car upholstery, crabs, ladybirds and mouthfuls of salt water, then evenings at Ted Johnson's oasis. The glorious, barnacle-encrusted rocks of summer rolled forever on.

"Even schools ain't what they used to be," Ted protested. "Back in my day, we made our own fun. Nowadays you just got crowds of brain-dead lemmings, all staring at their bloody mobiles. They're like life support machines to 'em. Take 'em away, they dunno what to do with themselves."

"You're blunt, but you've got a point," said Jock, smiling fondly. "When I was at school we passed handwritten notes around, with doodles and shit."

"There was this one time," Ted began. "A bunch of us spotted that the old caretaker who lived on the school grounds used to open up early for the teachers, then get 'imself back 'ome and put his feet up. Well, from that day on we realised that if we were sly, for an hour or so we had free reign of the school before the staff started rolling in."

"So what did you do?" Jock asked.

"We mucked around for a while, half-inching this and that," said Ted. "And then one day we found a raincoat in one of the cloakrooms, the kind that folds up into a tidy little plastic bag. You know? A cagoule."

"Yeah, I'm familiar with such all-weather accessories," Jock patronised.

"Don't get cocky, sunshine," Ted remonstrated.

"Sorry, Grandad," Jock laughed. "So what did you do with such a rare treasure?"

"We all pissed on it, until the bloody thing was saturated," Ted confessed. "The little bag was full of pee, and we were all falling about laughing at it. Then we raised the bar a little bitty bit."

"And did what?" Jock asked. "You shit in it?"

"Nah, that would've been *lowering* the bar, wouldn't it? Old mate of mine, Marky, well he grabs it by the little loop, doesn't he? We all caught on to what he was planning, and we ran like billy-o. Nuffin' like the threat of bein' bazookered with three other boys' piss to light a fire under your April, I can tell ya."

"Up to the point of hearing that story, my whole life has been a waste," Jock goaded.

"You may scoff," Ted continued. "But the almighty thunderclap of that thing hitting the walls in the corridor was enough to strike fear in anyone's heart. There's some considerable weight in a bag full of pissy cagoule. A direct hit would've knocked you flat."

Jock giggled contentedly. "Did you get away with it?"

"Yeah, course we did," Ted boasted. "Mind you, there was a right commotion over the giant patches of piss all over the school. I've never laughed so much in my life. We'd have wet our trousers if we hadn't all just 'ad one."

"Whose cagoule was it?" asked Jock.

"No idea," said Ted. "We never found out. Who's gonna own up to that one, anyway?"

"Makes my school years look tame in comparison," Jock enthused. "So what happened to Marky? Are any of the other guys still around?"

"*Life* 'appened, mate," said Ted. "People just drift apart, especially when girls come into the picture; then kids crop up. Colours fade to grey."

"Wow," Jock mumbled. "Just how long have you been all alone here, Ted?"

"'Ere, listen," said Ted. "If we're heading down that road, there's somethin' I need to tell ya."

"Sounds ominous,"

"Ominous ain't the word," Ted warned, and the ambient mood darkened forthwith.

After keenly arranging another round of drinks, Jock returned to his adopted spot on the dilapidated couch, eagerly anticipating this portentous chapter in the tale of Ted Johnson, irrespective of the lurid depths it could conceivably plumb.

"Come along then, Theodore," Jock enthused. "What's on your mind?"

"It's Frederick, you melt," he answered. "And before I go on, just understand that once I've unravelled this yarn you can't wind it up again. It's like a red pill situation, and it ain't no laughing matter either."

"Jesus, Ted. Sounds like it's you that needs to take a pill. What the hell happened to you?"

"I'm just saying," he went on. "Things 'appened that changed me, is all. And when I pass this missive on to you, well, it could affect the way you perceive certain fings."

"I tell you what," Jock began. "Following *that* introduction, there's no way I'm passing this up."

"No worries, squire," said Ted, sighing. "Well, it all started innocently enough, just like you when you wandered in 'ere. I was coming back from the pub, and it was raining. *Really* raining, like great big, fat drops that you could hear individually. It was warm, though, and the sky was full of lightning. But I didn't care none, I was ten sheets to the wind."

Ted began to relate the dark legend that had shaped his destiny and had eventually steered him to this unfortunately requisite juncture. It occurred in the field behind his current abode, bordered by a token perimeter fence and perpetually glazed with a sheen of stagnant water, at times riddled with frogspawn and Daphnia, and in the dark months, frozen hard. Negotiating the low fence, young Ted made his way across the marshy grass, spurning the abhorrent additional labour of circumnavigation in favour of picking his way across the quagmire. Already soaked to the skin by the unrelenting torrent of rain, it mattered little that his clothes and shoes amassed any further slurry due to his short cut. Amused by the innocuous sounds of his feet breaking shallow water and the consequent squelch as they freed themselves from the sucking mud, Ted found himself unusually calm and submissive, freed from the strains and anxieties imposed by modern society. It was then that everything changed. Right there in the pool of cold water, in the centre of the hoop of his engendered ripples, Ted Johnson fell to his knees amid a blinding volume of white light and the gentle pattering of rain. Familiar with tales of astral travel and the like, he was nonetheless agitated in the event of his own discorporate consciousness and its subsequent departure from Milk Field (so called due to its proximity to the old dairy). Becoming one with the odd luminescence until such a time as his cognizance was all that existed in this infinitely featureless white plain, Ted realized a state of panic, and it was during this episode of heightened clarity he was *shown* things.

Great biblical rains fell upon his known earth, chewing of the terrain, creating gulleys and tumbling rock. Lakes were formed within previously cracked and desolate basins, joining to create oceans into which swollen rivers sluiced their salty and destructive load. From the green-coated silt of dark and silent depths grew a voracious orange parasite, throttling and overwhelming with its limitless tendrils, poisoning the remaining earth and digesting its panicked stock. And still the rains came.

Inconceivable though it may seem, Ted was utterly convinced regarding the legitimacy of this possible future thronging its irreparable havoc through his captive mind; so it played on.

A forest of pale-lidded toadstools eddied with the restless waters atop fine orange stems from the ghastly, rapacious algae, sponging of the sun's energies that it might dominate the oceans and rivers that once were streets. Perhaps most terrible of all were the piscatorial abominations that carved through the bubbly depths with flashing grace, their faces bristling with obscenely repugnant tentacles to aid the conveyance of food to their sawtoothed mouths. Their cold and emotionless eyes were surrounded by textured gills, set into a soft head within a vaguely humanoid frame. Seemingly intelligent, these queer usurpers would communicate via the tapping and swirling of the fungi, its perky shades like light-dependent parasols on an incomprehensibly vast undersea network of organic transference. With hands like a knotted collation of sea cucumbers, they executed swift and complex symphonies upon the fungal lids, for all intents and purposes boastfully revelling in their oceanic conquest of earth, her remaining humans resigned to ardent survival on higher ground. Like savages, the formerly presiding race diminished to a dwindling and helplessly surplus resource, shivering in caves like a cataclysmic return to innocence while their television sets played host to bivalves. In the dark cold of the ocean floor, skulls of the righteous, the drowned and the beaten knocked almost imperceptibly against those of the wrathful and sullen, crying endless tears that flowed forever unheeded. The earth revolved within an aggressive film of water; this from the floating essence of an inebriate.

The gibbering and highly distressed Ted was deposited from whence he'd come, a foetal wreck within the splendour of an exquisitely moonlit pool of radiance and cold shock. He was in no quandary as to the authenticity of his vision, and it was etched into his memory as permanently as if the words of its legend were hewn into his bones. From sources unknown a secret had been delivered into his care; a disturbing vision of hereafter to which he was mother. Loath to haul his spindly form free from the marshy grass, he reposed among the tadpoles and whirligigs, blowing bubbles as his respiration steadied, as did his galloping heart.

Beneath a wonderfully clear sky of stars like pinpricks into divinity, the soak considered his epiphany, swathed in the milky glow of a pure moon. By all accounts, a moonchild lay immersed of his birthing waters and coated in mercury; a galactic messenger for the benefit of man.

Considering the absolute conviction with which Ted had related the tale of unlawful conquest and visitors from beyond the Milky Way, Jock was aghast, his doubting temperament scrambling for purchase to debunk such fantastical narrative. His aged host and raconteur appeared exhausted, a relaxed bag of bones and soft, atrophied muscle from which a great burden had been lifted. A runnel of hockle trailed from his pale lips to disappear into the iron-grey stubble at his chin.

"What did you do?" Jock demanded. "What happened?"

"Nuffin'," Ted whined, his voice reminiscent of a wheezing, asthmatic exhalation. "I drank, didn't I?"

"You drank? That's it?"

"Who'd believe that story, eh?" he squeaked. "D' you think the world was ready for the tale of old Ted who's fond of a few sherbets, and got 'imself abducted on his way home from the local?"

"Yeah, maybe not," Jock sighed.

"Exac'ly," said Ted, his thick glasses askew. "I drank to forget, and when I couldn't forget I just waited for it to kill me. The booze, I mean. Instead, it took everything I ever loved."

"How long ago did the abduction happen?"

"I dunno. Thirty years, maybe. Sorry to do this to you, sunshine, but that story's yours now."

"Wait a minute," Jock snapped. "What am I supposed to do with it?"

"Whatever you want to do with it, my son," said Ted. "I ain't got no right to any expectations. You're well within your rights to walk out of here, chuck it away and never think about it again, if you can."

"Fat chance," Jock admitted.

"Or you could keep the home fires burning. Tend the lighthouse, so to speak. Be ready for those 'orrible fings when they arrive if it's in your lifetime." Ted's hand slackened on his whisky glass.

"Nobody would ever believe that," said Jock. "It's like a bad dream. It's ludicrous."

"I know," Ted hissed, tan liquor soaking into the denim of his wrinkled, shapeless jeans. "I'm sorry, sunshine."

With a death rattle crackling from his tar-saturated throat, Ted was finally free of his apocalyptic burden. His glass tumbled to the patterned carpet with a curt, dulcet ring, settling by his slippered feet.

"No way, Ted," Jock urged. "Oh, you slippery shit!"

Bereft of his cruel and heavy penance, the oldest soak had slid out the side door and performed the ultimate bodyswerve, shrugging off his mortal coil lest his amnesty be rescinded. Faced with a sizeable quandary, Jock considered the option of assuming the mantle of learned soak, or deserting this entirely preposterous nightmare in the hope that time would erode its clarity, as would the wind and the quickening rain.

One thing was for sure, a stiff drink would almost certainly amend his outlook.

Tripper Treadmore and the Bloodsuckers from Maddison and French

(Coal-Black Limousine)

Before the emptiness of the extensive cul-de-sac just beyond the junction of Maddison and French Street there gently purred a slick behemoth of a vehicle, inside which there were shadows of such palpable density that little of the evil biding within could ever be discerned by such lowliness as a curiously meddlesome onlooker. Exuding the unusual fragrance of hand-warmed brass, the unnecessarily massive saloon was largely overlooked by the subservient inhabitants of Maddison and French and its immediate constituents. Thus, the predatory pursuits of all passengers and affiliates went unchecked for as long as any of the local sages could reluctantly and disconsolately recall. Far from the selective oblivions of the old town's majority, the spooky cult had attracted a consistent entourage of lowly teenage garbage since the days of zoot suits and pachucos, lured by the staunch appeal of something to break the monotony; an affront to the exhaustive, dogged conformity of everyday life, if you will. As the wind teased dervishes of sodden leaves, litter and specks of grit from the tarmac garage land forming the cul-de-sac, sending them on looping and endlessly bothersome flourishes around the square, self-condemning aspirants would approach the vehicle like nervous rats contemplating the raid of a lively refuse can. Peering in the narrow aperture of the open window, their inherent curiosities crucified them on beams of hunger, blood and the tantalising promise of eternal life. So the wheels of the abhorrent and eidolic vampire clan kept turning; ever teetering but roving with devastating denouement, nonetheless.

Having skulked and gambolled among the adjacent clutches of cockspur hawthorne, cleavers and foxtail grass, imagining pirates, renegade martial artists and hordes of the living dead for a rambunctious chunk of my wayward youth, and being blessed of a disposition bent on looking outside of *the box,* the activities of this curious clan had frequently stirred my errant suspicions. Moreover, the veil of hushed amnesty that the town afforded them galled at my righteous sensibilities like an irritant fibre snared in the lubricant juice of my eye; and it was with such long-tempered conviction and heroic yearnings that I was resolute in investing myself in the inauguration of their downfall.

My name is Dieter Pomme, and for years I'd worked hauling fifty-kilogram bags of sugar at the infamous Maddison Street refinery. I'll never be a millionaire, as one can conceivably project in the lowly roles of a servile donkey, but it put food on the table and provided me with a means to buy beer and maintain somewhere to drink it. Besides, it's not entirely unthinkable that one day far into the clouded future I can offer this lurid tale and its undiluted climax to the highest bidder, or maybe pen the entire chronicle myself. I'm not too shabby with the occasional adjective for someone employed as an obedient chimp.

Nobody in my immediate social sphere had fallen under the spreading cloud of these repugnant creatures' influence, yet I perceived their distant arrogance to be a most personal and caustic affront. Always the thieves and the scabby, stooped unwashed; the vicious and gap-toothed *diddly-donks* that hovered around the town centre in their tight little social knots that hearkened to the lure of this most illicit family. Far be it from misfortune that these disgusting reprobates were being systematically picked off from the once fairer streets, but rather a concern that they were being implemented into something infinitely more powerful and ruthlessly cunning. Upon my initial commitment to this foolhardy crusade, I began compiling notes in a jotter alluding to pertinent observations accrued on the everyday; at the outset, little more than a collection of disjointed scraps of overheard conversation, the occasional street name or public amenity and a dappling of names and titles. Over a period, one such denomination that recurred and resounded within my heart and bowels was the questionably virtuous moniker of *Tripper Treadmore*, a local bohemian musician and keen cyclist. Being of impressive and daunting stature, I opted, nevertheless, to afford him his own subsection in my investigative journal, and a sustained and covert pursuit of study therein.

I should mention, at this point, that my constant companion and steadfast confidante during these times was my girlfriend, Cheeky Peat. Tolerant of my passionate curiosity and vitriolic involvement in these studies and observations, she casually offered opinions and strategies, and acted as something of an informal director to my sinister creativity. Cheeky Peat was the glaze to my meat; the cleat to my rope, and the sweet wheat providing nourishment to my beat feet and fleet perceptions. Furthermore, her *backside* was shaped like a champion apple, and exhibited precisely the right amount of jiggle when she wiggled; but we digress. Her merits regularly exceeded wielding an exquisite behind, and she shared my misgivings concerning the gangly and shadowy fop that was Tripper Treadmore.

Of seemingly similar import was the frequency with which a particular sandy tower cropped up in blown whispers and idly rogue dialogue. Having lived my entire life beneath the shade of the unwritten politics strangling our town, then surely the only erection to fit such an unusual description was the old circular building out by the terminus of Heather Lonnen; a sweetly rural and ambient stretch of little bitty backroad frequented by cyclists, those seeking a spell of social amnesty and the odd. Provided the misplaced and mysterious legends were true, said building would be a certain test for the unwary, being surrounded by a quagmire of ploughed field and dilapidated farmland abandoned to rack and ruin, or rather a sucking marsh of hot mud, abrasive, gritty soil and despair. Such a place would serve as a resoundingly fine headquarter for nefarious activity, as in addition to its obvious qualities as a rudimentary watchtower, the cohesive swamp in which it was situated would betray any attempt at clandestine inspection. Without benefit of the capability of flight, not only would one's artless tracks be baked in the treacherous morning sunshine, but also the subsequent method and direction of retreat.

Nevertheless, between this pair of particularly pertinent clues I held two potentially prime avenues of investigation.

During this uncertain period of jeopardy and menace, I feel I must allude to languishing under the indefatigably steel embrace of a cold nightmare during which I found myself aboard a great and extensive haulage vehicle, the limits of which were such that they diminished into murky shadow. This cumbersome and impractical wagon was captained by a rodent-faced nag by the name of Dennis Lowdon, whose sallow skin was matched by his tubular teeth, concurrently presenting a sickly aroma, and leaving no doubt of impending death and preceding sickness in our capacity. Offering precious little in the way of assistance, he simply slugged from his tarnished tin flask, periodically unfastening the perpetually tortured and crooked hand-rolled cigarette from between his jaundiced gums. Between his bouts of slumber I was able to glean from him the urgency with which I was to unload this freight consisting of my life's worth of accumulated junk, most of which were a full-blown gut-punch of sentimental retrospect. Under the critical eye of our ochre-tinted host I surveyed racks of boxes and crates containing forgotten comics and toys of such poignancy that my efforts were further slowed under the heavy wealth of memories that wrung a sluggish tear upon my cheek. Regardless of this haggard driver's urgent schedule, the epic task of clearing this consignment of odds and ends and relics of dead friends was a half-day's work for a handful of men, and nary a solitary grunt, bent with the emotional encumbrance of his lost youth having returned from the ether.

To the crackly tones of a vintage rock band skirling from the radio in the driver's cab, I took the strain of my first box, the cherry on the top of which was a striped rubber ball with a dark singe, pliant to the touch, yet sufficient to yield an adequate bounce. Under sufferance of an infernally constant drizzle of rain somehow permeating this seemingly infinite trailer, the cardboard box conceded to the pressure of my grasping fingers like an aged dough. Conforming to the irregular shapes bundled within, the soft container buckled and soughed, and rifts evolved between haphazard straps of duct tape. The emphasis of this entire charade was overtly focussed on the embodiment of an eternal chore, or rather an insurmountable task. Slave to the illusion, I laboured on, hauling what was rapidly becoming a thick, soggy bag of yesterday's joys and aspirations.

As my palms were chilled from the damp fibres and my fingers bitten by the sudden revelations of stout and brutal copper-plated iron staples, so did Mister Lowdon become impatient with my rate of progress, casting glares and tuts filled with contempt and derision in the general direction of my troubled endeavour. Placating his scornful demeanour with a thin net of shamelessly regretful begging and apology, I resolved to double my efforts, attaining the wagon's rear door forthwith, and following many unlikely twists, turns and perilously narrow crevices. Setting down another of my traitorous treasure chests, I dropped to the ground and was presently beset on all sides by a fluffy cluster of large and friendly canines, their great smiling jaws offering nought but amicable attentions. At the helm of this small army of clouds happed with formidable tooth and claw was a hoary old man, impressively tall and long of beard.

"I'm afraid your dogs have me bang to rights," I extended, despite my most desperate restrictions with regards to time and toil.

No sooner had this exchange fled my lips than the most recently handled box containing a splendid collation of discontinued horror comics split with a report like that of tearing a great sheet of leather. The cardboard seams permitted a tide of irreplaceable literature and nostalgia to slough upon the deck, the fiendish folio therein smote on contact with the vehicle's deeply damp and unkempt floor. During a frantic melee of instinctive responses, my flailing arms propelled my funny bone to collide with a metallic projection, resulting in an immediate and all-consuming spike of pain. Then, even unto these bizarre proceedings, a most surprising course of actions transpired. The man, regal of mannerism and confidently aloof, lunged at my position and administered an unsolicited injection, jabbing an archaic-looking needle into my bad arm.

"I took the liberty of testing you myself," the dog handler announced in a voice like the rumble of a great many calamitous pebbles.

As my vision misted, weakly hindered by the overwhelming throb from my bashed elbow, I had only to wonder as to the fate of myself and my treasured belongings, forfeit for a second time in this preposterous string of events.

Henceforth, from one darkly surreal phase directly into another. Having pick'd my way throughout the twisting heathery lane that maintained an historically rustic ambience in an otherwise clinically modern and sterile town, I alighted within a stone's throw of the tower built from massive sandstone blocks. In the interest of stealth, I had pedalled on a bicycle equipped with hydraulic suspension rather than employ the explosive announcement of an internal combustion engine. The bike ride alone had been a magical and arguably infeasible journey.

Without the benefit of civil street lighting, I had coasted along a flat and gloomy straight; pleasant, were it not for the intrusion of a solitary bounding figure in the near distance.

Silent, was he; I knew this was so, for he was lit about the broad paps by the incident bleach of the full moon upon my guarded approach.

Without aggravation we passed in the night, heedless of one another, and I retained a notion of unreality in his passing. Surely in consequence of a phantasm, I'd have quaked in my saddle with the chance brush of an otherworldly apparition from the blind side of doom.

No sooner was this ghastly manner behind me than I was privy to further intrusion on my moonlight infiltration, as a most rare and fascinating oddity emerged from the forest of eddying stalks in the adjacent field. Believing it to be some imported form of *moon-monkey*, I doubted my own sanity upon observation of its protracted legs and awkward gait. Only as the animal made good its departure did I recognise it as a large and arrogant hare, the likes of which were scarce in proximity to such urban sprawl as the town that boasted Maddison and French. Simultaneously delighted in its natural reverie and its neutral stance regarding my mission, I closed the distance on the tower's stark projection, eventually wheeling my bicycle into the cover of a thicket of honeysuckle and coarse bramble.

Silhouetted against the great white dish of a buck moon, the round tower projected a portent of seething danger akin to a baited trap of grave consequence, its silence a deafening contrast to the soft whispering of the corn. Finding no alternative, I sank to my calves in the crusty mud moat, lapping and sucking of my cotton jeans, the cooling poultice providing scant salve, but rather depleting my resolve and passion toward the crusade against these parasites of the virtuous human essence. Cleaving clods of outrageous and sapping dimensions from the earth, I trod my way to within *hockling* distance of the tower's buttresses where the terrain relented to a softly yielding clay, as opposed to the sandy sea of earthen glue I had eventually and thankfully conquered.

Not even a sparrow did tweet as I regarded this sinister stone needle; a weathered oaken door between myself and its odious secrets, hanging askew like a brash affront to all that would consider its trespass and subsequent vilification. So tantalising were the suggestions of Easter eggs abound within the tubular belly of this aged folly, and so arduous and fantastical had been my short pilgrimage, that my enthusiasms were almost sufficient to grip of the unpretentious timbers and effect a solitary crusade. Nevertheless, respectfully cautious of the potentially malicious affiliates on the inside, I stayed my fervour and snuck beneath the door's cheesily fatigued and jagged grain. It was my opinion that this portal had remained untouched for some considerable moons, and if indeed this was some fashion of operational hive, then its infernally wily kin favoured the squint of the high windows as a mode of entry, against which only their specialist agilities and revolting clawed hands would prevail.

Once inside, my eyes trawled of the dense and sepulchral shade while my muddied jeans swept clumsy flourishes in the dank carpet of guano and sandy sediment, each soft scrape twixt man-made fibre and clotted dung amplified by the tower's stout concavity. Alone in the dark I waited, hunkered on my pulpit of mildewed manure, lest my enthusiasms yield to a reckless misfortune in anticipation of clearer sight and balanced mind.

As the filtered moonlight grudgingly revealed blurred details of the ground floor layout, I discerned a wealth of scrap and jumble; such a chaotic array of both household and industrial smithereens that I recalled a schoolboy refrain containing a narrative of *iron bedsteads and dirty old rags.* Despite the dire gravity of the situation I felt an instinctively masculine compulsion to salvage some token boon of possible future merit, because who knows when one's eminence should plummet for want of a corroded plough or a galvanised watering can filled with mice? In a suburb boasting this level of protracted depravity, who would object to the retreating figure of a bicycling man in support of a quantity of miscellaneous farm debris?

Opting in favour of self-preservation and sound logic, I stealthily approached a staircase hewn from further sandstone blocks and crude mortar, spurning the temptations of plunder to maintain my objective of initiating a sequence of events that would either condemn this repulsive, parasitic family, or at the very least compel the local public to address the deplorable knot of atrocities under which they were bound.

A glistening coat of green algae smeared the wall, encroaching on each step like a progressive disease, bumptious in its infinite patience and unwavering conviction to smother every stone within a softly debilitating embrace. Silently I ascended, my footfalls dampened by the prevailing lichen until I was afflicted by a most unrefreshing aura. Barely two thirds of these steps had I clumb before sufferance of an overpoweringly oppressive taint that chilled my flesh and seemed to oppose my every action with an invisible charge. Odd, that I hadn't so much as glimpsed a single animated soul but was primed with such an ardent conviction that unimaginable horror was poised in these upper levels, bent on the violent liberation of my precious blood. Amid this fresh and unique clarity of panic, and via the incongruous scent of a rare cologne, was I caused to consider an old acquaintance by the name of Jumper Smith, famed for his paper note of non-contribution with regards to the school's physical education on one particular day. Direct from his mother, it was alleged that Jumper was to forfeit the benefits of sport due to his sustaining a hernia in his foot. A far cry from the hilarity of Jumper's old bungle, the presence of his woefully acrid, yet unmistakable fragrance within these spoiled walls coincided with his cursory disappearance approximately two years past. That chemical abomination was sufficient evidence to reinforce my previously stalwart conviction that devils were at play in my hometown, and that the sandy tower out by the mouth of Heather Lonnen was now a confirmed headquarter.

Despite the absence of a physical compromise, I was more feart now than upon my approach, for now I veritably jingled with a richer bank of knowledge and would therefore present a more urgent and tactile threat to these shadowy fiends. Sliding through the inky blackness, I quickly facilitated my exit and kneaded my way across the choppy breadth of tepid, cloying mulch to retrieve my bicycle. Heedless of the adhering snails, blankets of dead leaves and curious caterpillars shaken free as I wrenched my wheels from their cover, I dove into the saddle and rattled my reckless way back to the adjoining road, glad of the fierce glare from the modern streetlights and the dubious solace of suburbia. Once home, my mind was a whirlpool of excitations and imagined outcomes to this one-way ride of toxicity and perilous justice. The glow of dawn had long daubed the halls and furnishings of my unfashionable home with her fiery tones of natural tenacity and hope before I was freed from my dreadful musings and granted the provisional oblivion of sleep.

So then the only prominent bone there remained to pick was the glorious smearing of meaty collagen that was Tripper Treadmore, the deliciously endearing and unconventional beatnik craftsman from outlying Engine Way. I fairly lost my blob to think of his affable reputation within the community, when beneath his garishly feathered hat there pulsed a snarled grey organ that had very likely masterminded the recruitment and inevitable conditioning of the feckless and bespectacled Jumper Smith.

Over the weeks and months following my observations at the sandy tower a lull descended upon the town of Parahoot'n like a thick fog, hindering our investigation as of a stout branch through the bicycle spokes. It was as though the devilish clan were alerted to our research and had gone to ground, no doubt in the action of cooking up some infernal plot to eradicate the meddlesome and pestilent itch I presented to their soft and partially exposed underbellies. It appeared that my little infraction hadn't gone unnoticed, and that my neighbourly concerns were not appreciated. In light of these developments I saw absolutely no option but to strike at that which manifested as the archetypal bogeyman ringleader. Tripper Treadmore had to die before any gnarled and clammy fingers came tootling their moribund means to myself and Cheeky Peat.

I hoped in the face of his downfall that his cohorts, rear guards and racketeers would be scattered in the wind for want of his patriarchal cohesion; divided and benign, their destinies to become as tar, blackened and liquefied, reclaimed by the earth in grisly atonement.

Forewarned is forearmed, as they say, and as such we were equipped for something of a gangland execution as we approached the Maddison Street refinery and its perpetual aura of citrus sweet cherries and deep brown mints. Within the soft folds of my jacket I cradled the bouncing bulbous balloon of flammable liquid that I hoped would facilitate the demise of our despicable mark. At my heel was the sweetly meek figure of Cheeky Peat, and her noxious tin clam of an overfilled petrol lighter, dangerously unpredictable in its wrath, and likely an item of some note to a collector of vintage tobacciana. Beyond the corner of Maddison and French there idled a black dragon's head in the more socially acceptable form of an infernally disreputable motor car, and I was determined that this day would be the last that its oily cough polluted the air and worried the town's children. About the great coaly freak there loitered several figures, one of which was the bunyip himself. Flanking the great and dandified tyranny of Tripper Treadmore were several token unknowns, and the insidious dwarf Stumpy Farrier, whose unfortunately cramped features would easily fit within the domed allowance of a common bread bun. Yet, this was not the day to permit the integration of such trivialities as intimidation and cowardice; now cometh the hour for a singular focus and gnashing of teeth, for the doling of justifiable agonies and the wilfully merciful letting of scoundrel blood.

On recognition of our approach the gangling bastard gestured with a carved cane, bone handled and wrought like a candy twist, and began a convoluted regurgitation of fractured rhymes and nonsense words; no doubt intended to bewilder and beguile the unwary, to charm and intrigue the callow or fond.

"All alone in his cardboard home, the preceding Rubbishfinger," he raved, effortlessly nonchalant. "Part'n young boys from their homes and toys was no job for a singer."

Dancing fleet of foot among his lesser brethren, Tripper Treadmore spake with the rhythmic nodding of a pansy snagged in his hat band. Little dreaming of an affront so brazen and reckless, he forged ahead with his scathingly apathetic airs against a backdrop of black metal and tinted glass, and the subtle, fairer tones of parlour music.

Swallowing my doubts and hesitations amid a spout of rising bile and the sour perspiration of impending cowardice, I strode to within handshaking distance of the beast and smote of my petrol-filled bladder upon his forrid, glazing his eyes with stinging fire and setting his hands to beat fruitlessly against the deadly implications of the chemical that saturated his hair and clothes. As I dodged beyond the sweep of environmental hazards, Cheeky Peat appeared from behind me, and she brought the devil.

Deftly, and with astonishing bravery, she snapped aflame the tarnished wick lighter and there spilled a tide of burning liquid from her hand. This she coolly tossed with the effortless poise of an Olympian avatar; utterly impulsive, yet sublime in its linear poetry, and while her feathered hair fell about her face in complimentary bangs of silken magic. The burning snarl of tin then bumped softly of Treadmore's cracked and scuffed bike jacket of calf leather, its casual kiss sufficient to enshroud him in a searing net of pain and a flashing, damning panic as he was engulfed in flames. Charged of a sudden and almost supernatural physical strength, I hastened to wrench free a length of steel palisade from a nearby abutment, triple-tipped with unforgiving spurs of a bitterly coarse and unrefined edge, and as he whirled and shrieked the most fearsome profanities, his loyalists dispersing in helpless angst, I skewered the black beast about the paunch.

Gouts of dark, glimmering blood were spewed upon my harrowed fingers, and with the steel shaft braced against the parish I hauled the imposing figure of the impaled Treadmore into the air, a macabre lollipop of seething inferno against the black-clouded sky. Such were the vibrations conducted through my rudimentary gallows that I could distinguish nuances in resistance as it was driven, tearing through a differential of gristle and tough, fleshy organs. Alas, so formidable was his hulk that my primitive partisan was cleft in twain and delivered his body to bump to the earth, leaving me clutching a subsidiary stub of wickedly jagged metal. Having transgressed the decent laws of man to this godless degree, so it galled me a great deal less to brandish my fractured blade, and with both hands stake the fallen braggart through his tainted heart.

Upon this most final and decisive violence, the former devotees ambled off as the great car spluttered into silence. Ostensibly indifferent, they wandered as soured children, bereft of their previous predilections.

I wondered, would the town afford us similar indifference considering our virtuous misdemeanours, as the coal black limousine provided *jazz* for the local miscreants with screwdrivers, adjustable wrenches and tin snips.

Mind Porridge

(An Introduction to the New Normal)

Upon garrulous reflection it appeared that this whole unfortunate saga had been an exercise in frustration; something of an enforced vacation in a series of elusively vital experiences. Young Danny was my *senior* by a handful of years, but the title he wore despite the lines on his gaunt face and his turkey neck that appeared to be hewn exclusively from elbow skin and scrotum. His new apartment, although hellaciously eccentric in its arrangements, impressed me a great deal. Upon initial contact it reminded me of an old community lounge in a sheltered accommodation that was part of my newspaper delivery route as a kid, thick with stale cigarette smoke and the underlying flavour of a wallpaper adhesive lacking the intrinsic ingredient that enabled it to set. It was a retrospective treasure, complete with a smattering of complimentary furniture fashioned from bends of steel pipe and discoloured sheets of laminated wood, etched with the fleeting human opinions of current moods during the transition between decades at the tail end of the 1970s.

Young Danny had asked me here under the premise that I'd assist him with the unappealing labour of toting his recently acquired chest freezer up a flight of hostile aluminium-edged stairs and into his spacious kitchen, although considering that he sustained himself almost exclusively on pots of fruit flavoured rice pudding, the whole affair seemed to me a most gratuitous and redundant gesture.

"What made you think this gigantic appliance would benefit you, mate?" I enquired. "You don't ever eat anything."

"I might," he answered, curtly; and that was our discussion concluded. I could vouch from long and bitter experience that any further inquisition into his decision to snag gargantuan kitchenware would undoubtedly lead to an aggravated rebuttal, and besides, his impetus was in all probability disappointingly mundane or otherwise absurd and worryingly perverse.

Leaving him in the lobby smoking hand-rolled cigarettes pinched 'twixt fingers tinged with pungent gold, I clumb the hostile stair to privately urinate before this lumbering endeavour could get underway. In keeping with the rest of young Danny's unusually disproportionate new apartment, his water closet was a grand and dusty chamber, borrowing its narrow dimensions from that of an empty railway carriage, yet with a sliding door and porcelain throne at one end; reminiscent of the final, indignant tooth in a gum that had endured great hardship and unjustified neglect.

I approached the pearlescent toilet in the customary manner, disconcertingly alerted to its coating of stubborn dust and tiny foreign bodies, and the occasional billowing of silken web in place of the customary body of frothy water, subtly tinted with a fresh, rural flavour or glacial tang.

As I stare into this bowl with chips,
I dream of life on boats and ships.
Of those who risk their lives at sea,
While I waste mine irrevocably.

Under the onslaught of my warm and absurdly chaotic stream, gossamer fronds were dashed and dissolved, becoming one with the flow while the film of sedimentary particles remained defiant in the absence of a more ruthless and solvent chemical. At the alarming tattoo of a thrumming, pattering moisture I was caused to punctuate my rejuvenating draught and investigate forthwith, as these were by no means a common consequence of *talking to Grandma slowly*.

Much to my chagrin I found the toilet to be isolated, and was therefore sluicing my foul water directly onto young Danny's unfashionably garish carpet. Protruding aggressively from the floor behind my ceramic nemesis was a wide vertical pipe, similarly decorated with a vortex of lacey webs and garnished with crumbling leaves, and into this hollow throat I noisily and reluctantly concluded my current business.

Returning to my temporary role as something of a domestic labourer, it aroused my sense of compulsive orderliness to see an errant margarine tub on a table, astray from the preserving properties of the refrigerator and likely prone to spoiling. As with young Danny's industrial deep freeze and cavernous *netty*, this container of low-fat spread was a beast, easily within striking distance of the title of *catering tub*. Beyond easy reach, I set about moving a chair that I might better effect its seizure, but was surprisingly stymied by a stout rope securing its leg to that of the accompanying table. Far be it from me to ponder the merits of knotting up one's furniture, I observed the attaching loop was of sufficient stringency that it should not be easily moved beyond the chair's rubber foot. At this, it became apparent that my intended act of altruism would be nothing more than an exasperating and ultimately futile gesture, and so I abandoned the rogue margarine in favour of hastily resuming our primary objective and leaving the infernally frustrating Daniel to his own peculiar devices.

Later that day it had been my intention to enjoy a cultured evening at the local theatre with my inconsistent companion Pip Kulick. Pip was a big old fairy, and despite our dissimilarities in sexual orientation I grudgingly admired him for his honest displays of submissiveness, typically cowing to the tyranny of his waspish boyfriend. Pound for pound, Pip could've snapped up the haughty little cunt like kindling and stowed him in his pocket for later consideration, a stark contrast to the reality of shooting me awkward and apologetic glances whilst enduring a vocal drubbing from this vitriolic gnome with a shit haircut.

"If I get back and you haven't used that money for the museum," ranted the queer.

Now, far be it from me to elucidate or intervene, but not only were we a woolly fifteen miles from the nearest museum, but the research and appreciation of historically significant artefacts hadn't been alluded to. I reasoned that this clarification would have been met with further malice from the salty punk, and maintained my silence, satiated in the assumption that intellectual calibre such as his would eventually lead him to a spell in jail or a similarly demeaning menial post.

Having eventually made our way to the theatre, negotiating slick puddles of ice and a dusting of frost like baby's breath, Pip and I were only too happy to part with our monies and be admitted into the warmth of the bustling foyer, having been supplied with our avant-garde admission tickets in the form of some beastly slivers of broken tile. Surely a curious and questionable quirk, it was nonetheless amusing to see the indigenous upper middle classes obvious displeasure at sullying their fingers with the grit of an authentic working-class token, likely fabricated under the sweating degradation of a chickenshit wage.

Already disheartened at the snooty clientele, and almost entirely convinced that this particular show had been a regretfully remiss selection, I tossed my ceramic nugget over the balcony in a gesture of indifference and managed to elude the embarrassingly subservient Pip in the process. Granted, this was an unforgiving and fiendish manoeuvre, but a justifiable one, I felt. The Pips of the world were content to be led by a strong and authoritarian dictatorship, and it was my opinion that said inequality required a sustained anarchic response to implement a mutually beneficial utopic equilibrium. Under current conditions the only things Pip Kulick could sustain were apologies, and so, regrettably, it fell to yours truly to attempt to derail him with these minor stinging injustices; besides which, his simpering mannerisms were really beginning to thoroughly gall my tit-end.

In keeping with the Dada precedent set by the chunks of masonry vended at the ticket booth, the stage was arranged before a network of stout pipes and geometric boxes and galleries, all strung about in a most ergonomically unsatisfactory manner. In order to fully appreciate the performance, and therefore follow the action in staunch fashion, one would be required to shimmy along the devilishly precipitous tubes in dogged pursuit of the ever-shifting optimum viewpoint. Adding insult to injury, a clutch of ripening *Nittany Lions* took to the stage and began their mournful rendition of some dated smash hits; eye candy for the forlorn and craven, but their sadly flapping tits and burgeoning thighs swathed in satin presented little to allay my overwhelming disappointment.

Hailing me from one of the vaguely dish-shaped geometric booths I spotted the local talent Lacey Beenshill, with whom I was familiar. Promiscuous and accommodating, Lacey was surprisingly good company with a decent line in cheeky gags and scant sufferance for fools. This salacious individual wasn't the type you told your mother about, but rather a delicious tale to be boasted when surrounded by a testosterone-heavy cloud of cigarette smoke, and comfortably boorish with the chaps. Respectfully celebrated and too fast for love, all the boys had an industrial-scale soft spot for Lacey Beenshill.

All things considered, Lacey's company may have been just what the doctor ordered and could quite conceivably have pared all the rotten bits off of a day hitherto squandered with the likes of young Danny and Pip Kulick, were it not for her unfortunate post. Had I the remaining tenacity and pluck to make her, I'd have had to engage in a very public display of death-defying balance and poise, scuttling along one of the immaculately architectured pipes until her sweetly pliant hands could fasten around mine and haul me aboard her seated pod high above the stalls. This alone was sufficient test without the distinct possibility of teetering precariously over a virtuous recipient of my formerly discarded tile. It wasn't inconceivable to fall buckled at the feet of some unfortunate john with a gashed crown or vexed eye because of my prior transgression, and thereabouts collect a deserved birching.

So it was with a resigning shrug and an apologetic gurn of ineluctably missed opportunities that I decided to conclude this day and chalk another one down to experience; and what fresh hell awaited me tomorrow?

For a few short months I'd shared a lowly bedsit with two other guys of personable character, and a mysterious old lady with whom I harboured no penchant or curiosity. A big old house akin to a student accommodation, it yielded each of us a private sleeping quarter and a shared kitchen/dining area. Above stairs was a spacious communal bathroom that smelled eternally of chlorine.

A fellow fitness enthusiast, Pump Sutherland braved the damp cold of the ground floor with me, while Stedge Butler and the old lady occupied the two upstairs bedrooms. Waking on the morning following the theatre fiasco, I resolved only to deplete my increasing heap of soiled laundry on this dreariest of days, compounded by the driving rain that coated everything in the dull and silty decals of flaccid fallen leaves. A limitless tide of mouldering, white-spotted seasonal litter, dashed in the unrefreshing ketchup of squished berries lending their bitterness to the incessant wash of abominably cold rain. A winter carpet; the decaying flesh of the sunny months we'd taken for granted, and now loathed in mourning.

Previously an ardent patron of the local launderette, I was consequently bent on learning the broad craft of home economics in order to better budget, and thence stuffed the machine's previously echoing cylinder with my mucid towels, socks and bloody, shitty underpants. This done, I was distracted by unsourced noises and left to investigate, having been convinced I was alone in my misery this foul and unequivocally brown and feculent morn. As it turned out, the old lady was the source of the unsolicited creaks and bumps, furtling around in her beige characteristic and paying my presence less heed than you would a spent match or a dead bird during your daily walk. Swaddled in her thick layers of a hickory nightmare, her coarse hair restrained in a soft and uncompromising net, she pottered around in zippy slippers as like a housemaid of the booming fifties, wholly immersed in an era that didn't concern me.

Reassured that these premises weren't host to any number of paranormal hijinks, I returned to the period kitchen, hung about with chunky bone-handled cutlery and with lard in a paper jacket, only to find a yawning cavity where the washing machine once stood, and my knickers strewn about the floor. What mode of hellish trickery was this, that had robbed a vital electrical appliance and left a crusty, mildewed aperture and flaccid pipes in its absence? Unsettled, though I was, I had little desire to succumb to the bad tide of madness and hysteria that threatened to overwhelm me. But then, how was it that my trusted housemates maintained wardrobes of sufficiently fresh and laundered linen in face of such insufferable subterfuge? Despite this phantom menace and its ridiculous precedents, I retained a dignified and composed front and readied myself to investigate.

Much to my vexation, a brief search uncovered a pump filter and various pertinent truck which my layman's eyes could not discern, and that were far beyond my limited skills to reassemble. So thoroughly perplexing was this turn of events, that when coupled with the absurd occurrences in young Danny's apartment and the Kulick theatre fiasco, my mind fogged with an entirely unwelcome broth of frustrated delirium. So intense was this phase of *fantods* that the contents of my bowels threatened evacuation, fetching tears to my eyes, and inciting my quaking hands to rip and tear beyond the restraints of socially lawful bonds. In any event, the oppressive atmosphere of this dated and crumbling excuse for a boarding house was affording me little incentive to regroup my scattered sensibilities, or to initiate a spell of personal reform and spiritual growth. In affront to whatever malicious assembly had brought about these unwarranted injuries of my psyche, I snagged my fraying and barely adequate kit bag and made for the gym. Perhaps a couple of hours of brutish grind would contribute to my mental recalibration, or at least distract me from the catastrophic living drown that hung threateningly like an intangible cancer.

The aforementioned gym, of which I was a dedicated and familiar member, was run by a bullish old bespectacled gentleman by the name of Wool Mason, and supplied exactly the kind of rustic ambience in which I felt at ease. Scant few of the machines and devices therein had arrived by means of a registered supplier, having been fabricated with great skill and fond care by the big man himself, deft behind the immaculate flare of an oxygen acetylene welder. For years had these unique and noteworthy apparatus been refining respectably chiselled giants with only a cursory glaze of physical casualty, typically the result of horseplay on the part of some particularly negligent baboon.

On this day Wool's was almost deserted, his peak time being early evening as those fortunate enough to be engaged in full time employment caned it to get home and fill their bellies before their fried eggs developed an almost impenetrable crust of stiff, coagulated yolk. Among the single figure collective was Benny Funk, a man of advanced years, acrid breath, and such satirically proportioned physique that his presence could almost have been considered a detriment to the gym's good reputation. Were it not sufficient that his perfectly spherical distended belly topped the most ridiculously thin and tubular legs, then one should consider his shit moustache; weak and farcical in its compliment of his rodent features, but a fitting accompaniment to his flagging wig.

Despite his physical handicaps, Benny was not only wont to dispense training tips, but to deliver them in an uncomfortably acute proximity. Otherwise outwardly inoffensive and personable, whatever aspect of Benny's character that compelled him to invade a man's personal space to an almost sexually suggestive degree during conversation was thoroughly abhorrent. It was with flogged resignation, therefore, that my arrival was cheerfully acknowledged by the misshapen Benny Funk, and a further assault upon my battered will at his suggestion that I join him in *leg day*.

As had been my singular motivation, a spell transpired during which I was distracted from the *mind-porridge* of my daily intercourse via the dubious gift of rubbery quadriceps and hamstrings threatening to cramp. Were it not for Benny's gastric halitosis and the lamentable plight of his combover, I should have deemed it a pleasurable afternoon.

Engaged in the cockpit of Wool Mason's commendable leg press machine, toes turned outward to further aggravate my previously distressed semitendinosus, I pressed for my queen and country, this being my final set of repetitions before heading off to reassess my earlier debacle with the washing machine. To my surprised indignation there came a metallic crash like the terminal fall of a guillotine blade that set my ears to ring at its overwhelming peal. It seemed I had inadvertently supplemented Wool's accident statistics in completely severing an already frayed cable, fetching the ample stack of iron resistance to crash atop its oily brothers. Suitably abashed and visibly shaken, my anxieties were exacerbated as the resulting tremors dislodged a considerable splinter of cracked glass from a nearby transom light to shatter by my station. Across its shivered slivers in broad strokes of ink was the moniker MICHELLE, which held little resonance with me, I'll ashamedly admit.

Should even the gym rebuff my sanctuary, then where remained for me to roam?

Following the week of self-imposed rest and recuperation that had produced such innumerable disasters, I was relieved to be returning to work, and having restored the washing machine at great detriment to the leisure times of Pump, Stedge and myself, I was able to don my work clothes amid the fresh fragrances of vanilla and sandalwood. Needless to add, assistance of any kind from the freakish old cat lady were found wanting, although she continued to benefit from the communal appliance in its return to form.

To my mind, there's something earthy and utterly respectable about holding down a menial occupation such as the post I shared with Patrick Ball. When I clocked out every weekday afternoon, threading my way through the idling crowd of *pigs* (as they were disparagingly known), it was with honest blood caked on grazed knuckles and blue-collar muck ground into the fabric of my fraying jeans. Although we considered ourselves worthy to patronise and deride *the pigs*, Patrick and I were superior by only the very narrowest of margins. Within the factory's many boundaries, and consequently the company's influence, these were the disposable, entry-level grunts of varying pedigree and capabilities, whereas we were responsible specialists; *trustees* of a fashion. As the product (irrelevant at this juncture) was assembled and meticulously boxed for the consumer, it was thence our business to wrap it in a waterproof protective layer atop a wooden pallet of specific grade. These units were then labelled, logged and stored, and their relevant paperwork passed on to the self-dubbed *warehouse sex offenders* for dispatch. For the most part, aside from the general hubbub of frenetic and boisterous activity, the little oasis of our finishing department afforded us limited peace and privacy to better milk our negligible privileges; specifically to engage in horseplay beneath our umbrella of exaggerated self-importance, and to flout the prohibition of electric mobile telephones.

This day, on the debut of my return to occupational form, there came a distant rumbling; a formless, chaotic cacophony, the likes of which set my flesh to crawl at the irksome feature of quarrelling masonry and steel. Patrick (the bumbling Santa Claus of Cowley Park) and I hastened to investigate and were met with a chilling fancy to quash our perfectly natural curiosities.

Neither of us could believe our stricken eyes, although Patrick appeared content to ween this was the culmination of an elaborate practical joke. No less than a headless suit of

Elizabethan armour roamed the scuffed and skid marked shop floor on company time, and pushing a metal container on bested castors.

A quintessential jockey of mirth and frivolous gratitude was Patrick Ball before this potentially supernatural vision, but for me, an unwelcome cranial pressure developed in conjunction with an almost total loss of coordination and bitter tang.

Oft times reality is stranger than fiction. Sometimes a great deal.

Pepper Siege Three
(The Short Flare)

Before foundations were laid for the now sprawling housing estate of East Action, there stood two houses within a stone's throw of each other, both unique and unaffiliated. Each with a riverside view, their property lines skimmed the invisible boundaries of the derelict Len Colliery, relics of which were still highly accessible to those with an eye for post-revolution history; a spot of natural splendour since the reclamation of the dark soil to the unrelenting appetite of a wealth of indigenous shrubbery and associated wildlife. Indeed, so prodigious were the clutches of giant hogweed that one could quite conceivably become disorientated amid their colossal flourishes. Their toxicities were such that a touch or a brush could induce a rush, an incendiary blush; a rash or a blister, persistent insister that ne'er an opportunist belonged in this scrub.

Aside from the venomous properties of few, the obvious glory of nature's palette and the unhampered scent of fresh blooms tended by the scarlet wings of the six-spot burnet moth were a tonic and a gift to curiously little, although certain secluded features periodically inspired the curiosities of the parish children. Ponds had formed as a natural consequence of subsidence, and their living bounties delighted goodly youngsters equipped with makeshift fishing nets and jars tied with string as the shifting of the seasons heralded their spawning.

Perhaps more manifest had been the formidable monument formed by the caching of uprooted sleepers from the former colliery railway track. This imposing haphazard pile of deep and epic timbers was the unexplored ruin of a routed civilisation in the eyes and imaginations of many a child with the smit of creativity. To others it represented fuel; tinder of the gods, fit to kindle a blaze with sufficient volume and passion to set the world on fire, were it not for their density and thirst. Such was their saturated condition that the town was stung for the glory of a pyre, despite the best efforts of a token troop of grubby-fisted ragamuffins with a few scavenged matches. Soon the vast lumber was gone and recalled by few; so peppered was the terrain with ravages and scraps, and the river licked of its black sand, nourishing its odd crustaceans.

Parted from the traditional myths and wonders of the Len Colliery wastes by means of fences of varying merit and design, the two houses were occupied by three individuals, yet despite the contradiction of their reclusive proximities, the clans seldom exchanged favour. The first that should afford closer examination was occupied by a brooding and shovel-handed chap by the dashing title of "Kid" Nicky Skyfire; hardly the type to invite social engagement and merriment, his enigmatic airs were further cemented in his succession of the property from a beast of ill repute. The fiendish pursuits of the former resident of number three, while no doubt wildly embellished and primped by the outraged townsfolk, were rooted firmly in fact, and despite having had no affiliation with the shadowy *Mister Sindy*, the taint of the land's former nature threw ignorant speculation about the knotted shoulders of Kid Nicky. Ordinarily a personable gent, a useful prize fighter and upholder of respectable morals, his voluminous, curling moustache betrayed an ornery and subversive streak in the eyes of the locals; yet he remained unabashed, for their archaic manner and fragile composures held little interest for him. In so far as perversions, Skyfire had in his possession a polythene bag containing an enviable assortment of second-hand adult interest magazines (stroke books) that he'd been amused to find during an exploration of surrounding thicket and meadow one fine afternoon. Tucked away in his private chamber, their garish celebrations of femininity presented something of diversity from the deviant appetites of Mister Sindy, *his* penchants running into the chaotically exotic and criminally licentious. In comparison, the thick glossy fancies of Kid Nicky's plastic bag were but a slip of a cupid's arrow. And besides, his absolution in the ultimate sacrifice loomed tantalisingly beyond his perception like the traditionally recognised figure of death; all-consuming, glowering darkness and the barbed, serrated absence of mercies.

Hard and durable as the proverbial pea in a tin whistle, Skyfire rattled echoingly about the mysteriously reticent horror house conducting his own business in a bland and peaceable manner, and so we adjourn to the somewhat grander adjacent property occupied by the Peppers.

Having been maintained with a more meticulous and constant hand, the Pepper house presented a fairy-tale front of soft and rustic majesty, incorporating a ramshackle barn and robust tree stump, cleft with a woodsman's axe following a spirited chopping quest, and bedecked with fallen blossom.

The Peppers themselves were Roy and Kent, bereft father and daughter, and textbook example of soap-operatic life, replete with all the first-world problems of a family loathe to acknowledge its remaining virtues.

Kent was a princess, a natural beauty with a halo of golden hair and the instinctive misapprehension that the world owed her favour for such as the splendour of her pliant pink lips and flashing eyes. To her credit, the glossy lips *were* spectacularly enticing, yet insufficient to satisfy the outstanding deficit of compassion and humility for which she was found wanting. Her father, the browbeaten piggy bank Roy Pepper, was a balding old lump of suppurating self-pity and loathing with a distinctive diastema, or *chapper* between his front teeth. Such was the extent of said gulley that deep in the decrepit well of his glum recollections there festered memories of being hunted for the express purpose of having sterling currency forcibly wedged into the gap. His flannel-trousered schooldays were remembered for being Roy Pepper, the kid with a chapper you could fit a *threepenny bit* into.

Having channelled the indignities and frustration of his school years into developing his skills as a shrewd and ruthless opportunistic investor, Roy's numerous bank accounts were comfortably swole, while his city hands remained as fat and doughy as his grey-haired tits. Though his ample stomach and greeting-card cottage belied a utopian existence, his was a life of constant stress and grief, moving heaven and earth to meet the high-maintenance expectations of the brattish cunt that was Kent Pepper.

From below his beetroot nose, amid the busy bottles of half-finished spirit, the soothing, dulcet tones of afternoon radio whirled and floated by the peeling green paint of his kitchen door and out into the wonderfully refreshing air of the rural strip. Awash with pollen and the salty humidity of the nearby estuary, his garden boasted floral vines abound throughout the beaten trellis and the charm of the twisting path; those little cracks and slivers of flag and tile, overgrown and supplemented by the endless, soft fall of exhausted petal, their delicate silence a veil for the invasive vulgarities of the barn.

For within those weathered timbers, a damage on sweet fairness.

Whose poison footsteps fate would lure outwith these folks' awareness.

In the belly of the endearing page of history that was the Pepper barn there reposed three sickening chancers around a gently smouldering fire, its tempers subdued so as not to arouse suspicions regarding their presence and subsequently hostile intentions.

By far the most striking of the three was the sole female, known by the name of Hunter. In unmerited contrast to her sociopathic tendencies she was possessed of an arresting, almost feline beauty, and a cascade of soft, chestnut hair to frame her flawlessly handsome visage. To label this vile succubus as attractive or pretty was woefully inadequate; Hunter was stunning, such that your greedy eyes would be sucked from your head on fraught stalks and your jaws left mumbling feebly. Her glossy black leggings (a chic short flare, ending in a ruffle about the calf) displayed a set of broad hips upon which all others should be modelled and found lacking; and not to beat the notion into the ground, but those black-clad winning thighs were so slick that they resembled the liquorice pipe component in junior smoker's kits supplementing eighties Christmas stockings all over Britain.

Hunter was a dangerous animal, the more so because of her unlearned disposition and general ineptitude; but with an appearance like hers, who needed smarts? In the kind of seedy underworld circles dependant on the integrity of such as this deviant trio, sex was a readily acceptable currency, and Hunter fucked everyone like it was sharing sweets; everyone, that was, except for Pip Kulick.

Pip was a big guy; big like the old parlour trick of setting someone on your shoulders and you both getting wrapped up in a fat man's overcoat, and his wiry, bristling hair made him look taller. Far from being as dumb as Hunter, he had a diminished, bookish intelligence that you'd almost perceive as discomfiting, should you ever catch him engaging it during a lapse of character. If ever a man was perilously crazy, it was Pip Kulick; those anxious eyes of his never fully collaborated with the expression he was wearing, like somewhere in between there was a little bitty gremlin jabbing a screwdriver into his circuitry just to see the sparks. It was a most lamentable transgression of chance that he'd fallen in with this unsavoury shower of piss and villainy, yet true to form he'd found himself roosting with another boss figure, a salted whip for his docile and mechanically subordinate haunch in the form of John John Ormston.

Ormston was as foul and contemptible as any bad guy can get, a claim plainly substantiated by the maudlin kitty-cat glowering from the shadows, the barn ailing for the tang of burnt fur as her tiny litter popped and crackled, blackened aflame by his wrathful, barbarous hand. Reckless, cowardly and mean, he aspired to the colours of the American OG genre; all pistols, hoods and ill behaviour, though the pronounced overbite he carried on his balding melon head rather alluded to *original vampire* than a hardcore player from the streets of Watts, Los Angeles. His beetling black eyebrows complimented sunken cheeks and overlong, unkempt teeth, all suspended on a stooped and crooked neck; a fitting focus to a backdrop of full moons, rubber bats or a knotted batch of squabbling rats. Yet despite his wiry, gothic aspect, he maintained a keen survival instinct and a lowly streetwise intelligence that manifested a perfect marriage of criminal deviance and pure, daredevil pluck.

Nothing but an unfavourable collusion of ill fate and the whims of the dastardly, then, that these generally challenged and downtrodden offspring of an impoverished generation should establish an entrenchment in the Pepper barn; drinking, blazing up the bubonic chronic and poppin' off some dope freestyle shit as they anticipated nightfall, and the usurping of a suburban nirvana.

> *When I was frontin' on the streets, yo, I got beat down,*
> *I was broke, but I never was complete down.*
> *I got to lyin' and I's stealin', and I cheat down,*
> *I got a stone cold rep and packin' all the heat now.*

Darkness fell with all the palpable intensity of a clement Halloween garnished with a fine mist from the estuary, and the abysmal party of pigs finalised their plans amid the pissy steam of their extinguished fire, its cracked eggshell skulls pilloried and wretched. John John's speculative theory was that the unarmed occupants of Pepper cottage would be overwhelmed via the application of minimal tussle and harsh language, and that the employment of firearms and bladed weapons should be considered as a last resort. Since he held the only gun (a reconditioned service revolver), there should be minimal opportunity for anyone losing their composure and Peppers gett'n *sprayed* as a result. Of course, one couldn't discount the probability of the highly agitated and volatile contributions of Hunter and Kulick, whose unpredictable characteristics could quite conceivably reduce this common or garden domestic armed robbery into an abortive farce with the sudden introduction of a concealed blackjack or a shank. Those were the risks when embarking on a life of petty larceny and extortion, not the least of which being the involvement of such low-level toxic *loonies* as the Pepper siege three.

"Just keep a level head," John John enthused.

"Right," said Kulick, nodding nervously.

"That little bitch gives me any shit," Hunter added. "I'll kick her cunt up her back."

"There ain't gonna be any reason for anyone to get excited," said John John. "No-one's going to jail. Believe me, I'd love to give these silver spoon motherfuckers a spell in a wheelchair, but this heist should be easy. In and out. Nobody moves, nobody gets hurt."

"Right," added Kulick.

Deplorable directives processed, the calamitous party departed the barn under cover of shadow and thicket, the aged barn door warping and flexing weakly under duress of their passage. John John assumed the role of point man, indicative of his faith in the desperate assemblage, and taking full advantage of the low hanging blooms to conceal their ill-fated approach he tiptoed through the settling dew. Negotiating the abstract paving with its dips, bevels and borders of worrisome weeds and hardy grass, they reached what was affectionately known as *Nana's rain barrel,* an imposing plastic drum filled with an organic broth of rainwater, algae and natural decomposition, and home to all manner of intimidating, hovering, segmented beasties.

"I can't wait to get back to fucking civilisation," muttered Hunter.

"Just keep it down to a dull roar," John John hissed, opting against the implementation of an hilarious anecdote regarding Hunter fucking *all* of civilisation. As it were, such jocular quips would most likely be lost upon integration with the limited communication capabilities of Lynette Hunter.

Reclining in his not-inconsiderable underpants regarding the twisting flames of his sparking, snappy natural log fire, Roy Pepper melted into the supportive embrace of his favourite chair, drinking of the delicious ambience, and of his aged Scotch in its amber majesty. Lending his fishbelly-white surplus to every nook the chair presented, he considered his lifetime achievements and his conquests of late, striving to assuage the voracious, gluttonous demon of self-loathing and bitterness; to tamp down its virulent head, lest it begin to wail and gnaw of his precarious sensibilities, running amok throughout the delicate equilibrium of his mind and making his nose to bleed. As the soothing spirit calmed him, cooling his charging blood and affecting a measure of peace about his furrowed brow, he became increasingly dismissive of conventionally suspicious creaks and bops, as they were almost certainly benign characteristics of this old house settling under the chill of night, and the tiny woodland folk of lore conducting their nocturnal affairs via the medium of magic and dance.

Oh, hallowed desolation, my eternal companion.
For under your regard I am truly free from judgement and derision.
Unto you my heart is bare, my frailties exposed.
Let's bind them together, in lashings of hope.

As knotty pine popped and spat atop his fire to eventually fall as sparkling embers in a bed of anonymous ash, so did the Pepper siege three tackle his barely adequate rear door lock and gain ground within the formerly tranquil kitchen. Plastic shoes of brilliant white betrayed their presence, eliciting traitor barks of alarm upon thick, regal tiles as the sanctity of the home was soured by these irreparably repulsive creatures. Such was the tattoo that the serenities in which Roy Pepper reposed were finally interrupted and his startled curiosities piqued, to the uproariously rash extent that he grabbed for the drawer of his felt-lined walnut cabinet where some of his fondly-maintained modified Derringer pistols were stored. Snagging a wonderfully engraved filigree model, he hurriedly confirmed its charge and prepared himself to fire. Despite the painful leaps and twists his overtaxed heart was currently performing, the slight mass of the pocket pistol sat reassuringly well in his hand, and despite all the fears and pertinent moral complexities, the opportunity of discharging his weapon with lethal intent under the consideration of home security was markedly exhilarating.

There came a mumbling from beyond the kitchen door, an indecipherable organic hum of the most crude and basic English, following which the golden curve of the door handle was engaged and gap-toothed Roy observed the subsequent void of the scullery breached by a most awkward and loathsome misfortune of nature. Ferociously defiant in the extensive weave of his Y-fronted briefs, he fired at the inquisitive, rodent countenance of John John Ormston, and by an arguable stroke of good fortune the slug found its intended mark. With a resounding clap and a snarl of smoke there occurred a puncture, like a ladies' piss-hole upon his neck, and the young villain was to bear a mask of consummate surprise and wide-eyed bewilderment as he stumbled, to eventually collapse in a gurgling, croaking heap of gouting blood and flouted opportunity. The Pepper siege had incurred its first fatality.

Startled awake by the gun's sudden report and ensuing mayhem, Kent Pepper rapidly adopted the unenviable guise of the panic-stricken maiden, an unappealing, self-devouring vortex of streaming cosmetics and air-propelled snot. Yet, having the presence of mind to remain silent so as not to betray her whereabouts, she shed her inappropriately diaphanous nightgown and dragged on a pair of jeans.

Tears a-streaming, she hoped she were dreaming, as the face of her father yelled up through the ceiling. He screamed and he choked, things crashed and they broke. Old Pepper the nepotist done got himself smoked.

Now, farbeit from fate to apportion worth to the remaining members of this disreputable glee club, but they fairly flew at the fat man in the underpants at the disintegration of their fiend-faced, chinless leader. Dramaticised with the cinematic wonder of slow-motion video and accompanied by some bold and stirring overture, the entire scene could have garnered some noteworthy acclaim, and elicited such enviable reflections as *powerful* and *important*.

Hunter fairly flew at the tubby shootist, the scene of her dark trajectory enhanced by a grim countenance within a maelstrom of glossy locks and a fluttering murder of textile ravens. Among the lethally hypnotic frenzy there glimmered a serrated blade from Pepper's own kitchen; it had never been used and therefore retained an exemplary edge, a factory standard that positively hungered for the deliciously cathartic parting of meats. Pip Kulick concurrently furtled about the remains of the Ormston debacle, eventually snatching of the aforementioned service revolver and bringing it to bear on the moribund arse candle that was Royston Temple Pepper. With a flare of deafening fire and a most unrefreshing jolt upon his stout, but largely untravelled wrists, Kulick shot their unwitting nemesis in the thorax; not quite the instant kill he'd have been drilled in basic training had he joined the army, but a sufficiently lethal injury, nonetheless. The lamentable form of Roy Pepper folded and was beset by the virtual army of dubious personalities called to arms by the recurrent dominance of bleak Hunter.

Mounting the crippled and bleeding obstacle, she hacked and slashed with a horrifying frenzy, her eyes feral and intractable pits of dumb rage. With indiscriminate abandon, the face and neck of the fallen Roy were shorn and sliced until his eyes lolled, useless ruptured organs beneath irreversibly mangled lids, cleft and scooped and torn by a perfect edge.

The knife continued to rattle its flashing scallop over his teeth and gums, raising little crimson runnels that would sap his weakening body and further panic his struggling heart. An overstep with regards to penance for his arguably righteous termination of John John Ormston, Roy Pepper would expire beneath the long and shapely thighs of Lynette Hunter, who'd incidentally pissed herself. Under more general circumstances, a gentleman's revelry to be gripped between such sodden and milky hams, warmly pliant like a deliciously living dough; but in this season of wither this crime would be delivered under censorship to an eager and ghoulish public and would still raise many a hot-blooded fellow from his bed to reaffirm his locked doors at night. For now, irrevocably lost in an appealing blanket of confusion and shock, Pip Kulick simply pumped his fists, eyes glazed as if he were twenty-seven beers deep and swallowed up in a throng of merriment at the local bar.

It was with all haste, then, that the reservedly resplendent Kent Pepper departed the comparative safety of her private chamber and burst into the nucleus of this unmitigated catastrophe armed with another of her father's Derringers, the locations of which he'd insisted she marked, and with evidently good reason. Oddly attractive with her streaked mascara, she scowled seven years of refined loathing into the mounted form of Lynette Hunter before taking aim from the stairwell and shooting her in the shoulder, the report of which brought the remaining assailants to attention and altered the dynamics of the fray somewhat. Slumping forward upon Roy's mutilated carcass as a result of the gunshot, Hunter was allayed from her current labour of butchering the dead man's considerable rump, a whopping slab of which was almost completely severed.

The inconsolably hysterical Kent, overwhelmed by survival instinct, made a break for the door at the foot of the stairs, keen to withdraw from the helter-skelter nightmare into which her father's drawing room had descended. Her cold, quivering fingers betraying her in the act of disengaging the lock, she gibbered and raged, rattling of the chains and bolts in a desperate bid for self-preservation, and to the tune of Hunter's demented resolve.

"Catch that shame of a cunt!" she demanded of Pip, jolting him from his frivolous musings as he dithered by a dated wingback armchair; a missed opportunity in its cheering promise.

And so the end began; a chase ensued, the likes of which Kent Pepper could never have previously imagined. Having eventually solved the trembling riddles of the front door lock, she fled into the still of the night, its immediate balm delivering a welcome boost to her rasping lungs, their stale contents a queer mixture of death, sweat and a most baleful revulsion for the degenerate maggots that had invaded her home and slaughtered her father.

Under sufferance of a dry spell the earth beneath her feet was baked hard, compacted and cracked, and whilst providing great traction it jarred of her skull in response to her awkwardly discombobulated footfalls, as such were her legs that they were driven purely by a natural desire toward survival, their bones thumping rigid on watery muscles. Her eyes were thrown wild like wilful thrill seekers in a careering tractor tyre, and her view was partially obscured by her unfettered, windblown locks as behind her, the deeply disturbed and impressionable Pip Kulick gave chase, gunning from the lighted porch like a wild dog.

The tall flora and trees she'd celebrated under more agreeable circumstances were suddenly stony and ignorant of her plight. Despite the shelter she'd previously taken beneath their rich boughs, or how she'd appreciatively traced of their unique intricacies, they spurned her tearful desperation and simply *were*. Her unwarranted exile seemed absolute and irrevocable, were it not for a beacon of amicable warmth winking faintly from the former property of the objectionable *old man Sindy*, and now the residence of that big old buzzard with the moustache like a great stringy croissant balanced on his split lip.

As the great, milky moon lapped of the estuary's black waters and dappled of its faux frost upon the land, Kent fled carrying a crumb of hope to which she clung like barnacles on a breached hull. Should the gangling loony close the gap between them then the battle was most certainly lost, and barely worthy of the term conflict; surely then would it be referred to as the *massacre* or *bloodbath*, and this forlorn daughter of Roy Pepper would be demoted to a typically faceless crime statistic, and nary a deserving survivor or champion of the Pepper siege three.

Coarse, spade-like blades of grass lashed at her feet, and spiny brambles throttled her ankles, encouraging rosy beads of blood to bloom on her exposed flesh while her clinging threads became an encumbrance, laden with an accursed brew of dewy perspiration and the bodies of tiny flies caught up and mangled in this chaotic misery. Though one could certainly be tempted as a reaction to her formerly uncharitable nature, her staunch heart should bear no criticism; the delectable Kent

Pepper was far beyond driven, whether in the interests of justice or simply an indomitable will to survive. Though her generally lustrous and golden ringlets clung to her skull in a solution of saline snot, and her radiant skin bore the flushed hallmarks of farthest agitation, her canvas-clad feet bore her ever-onward in pursuit of the big man's porch and its perceived sanctuary outwith the thundering boots and grasping arms of the Kulick hobgoblin. Seemingly unhampered by the niggles that so heavily dogged the dear Pepper girl, Pip crashed through the undergrowth with a great many unpalatable ventures on his agenda; be it the gratification of sheer physical dominance or a darkly sexual indulgence without the customary restraints of a consensual party, he cared not a jot. In his capacity as an associate of this awful, bungling criminal enterprise, he'd been self-conditioned as an unappreciative, barbarous thug, and had been moderately successful in his endeavour. Pip Kulick's perilous lack of direction had beggared a humanitarian audience, but instead he'd assumed residence within something akin to the infamous Spahn Ranch, and replete with its own rancid family of catastrophic malignance.

Through eyes blurred with tears and a great many sidelined aggravations, Kent closed in on Skyfire's stoop, pleasantly decked with quintessential rocking chair and a humming electric bulb, tarnished with the singed dust of a thousand moths and beacon to a thousand more, heedless of the pyre of immolated corpses on Nicky's rough boards. Similarly, Kent flung herself at the mercy of what could ne'er eschew the dark taint of Mister Sindy, and the porch rail obligingly stung her with some barbed and substantial *spelks*, the likes of which were a trifle considering the bigger issues.

She fairly pounded at the wooden portal and brayed the ghastliest keen which had, in embryo, been an arrangement of syllables that tangled and jumbled 'twixt motive and engender.

Should the unwitting hero be otherwise engaged in such pursuits befitting a bruiser whose interests included the competitive fisting of boorish men within a hay-bale enclosure, then all would be lost in Kent's detention, subsequent molestation, and probable dismemberment. As it were, her cacophonies were acknowledged on the double by the anxious, lunar mug of "Kid" Nicky Skyfire, the very sight of whom induced such a cataclysmic rush of solace within her pert and springy bosom that her knees fell weak and she wept fitfully, punctuated by circumstantially sincere pledges of personal reformation.

Kid Nicky's round, caser head registered immediate perplexity and concern for the listless wretch that had fallen at his mercy on the rustic decking, such that when Kulick arrived in a veritable cyclone of barely coherent mutterings, thundering boots and the consequential rending of cumbersome shrubbery, his execution of frontier justice was swift and severe. The unprecedented confrontation of a freakishly tall man (snorting, and with bug-eyes) in evidently unlawful pursuit of a distressed waif during some dark and ungodly hour warranted stiff reprimand under the old-school book of regulations to which he accorded his principles, and as Pip Kulick veered onto the porch via the central pivot of Nicky's weather-beaten newel post, he met the dukes of *hazard*.

Reacting instinctively, Kid Nicky delivered the old one-two to Pip's unshaven, horsey face; a slick, almost balletic manoeuvre from such ham fists atop arms like telegraph poles enshrouded in flesh. The effect of the left jab, right cross combination was a multiple of what it would've been had Kulick been a stationary target, and not running blindly onto Skyfire's answer to *Suzie Q*. The upshot was that Kulick was momentarily airborne, sailing from the porch to be dumped on the rough and overgrown cobbles leading down toward the river, where his already dazed and unworldly noggin cracked like a nut.

The twisted and dismal misadventures of Pip Kulick leaked from his split melon and were greedily absorbed by the loamy soils, gumming the spindly legs of all the ants that dwelt in the cracks; a far cry from New York City, yet the sparrows would still sing in the morning. Without so much as a deep inhalation or labouring heart, Kid Nicky's journeyman knuckles had mangled his face to the degree that he appeared to be caught in the perpetual act of attempting to blow a bothersome fly from his lips.

Skyfire turned his attention to the yellow-fleeced refugee that was curled by his feet, and scooped up her softly malleable deadweight after hurriedly wiping a dead man's rheum from his fists. Once inside the building that was theoretically cleansed of all Mister Sindy's indecencies he could administer basic first aid and offer alms until such a time as the emergency services would relieve him of his unwitting responsibility. Abandoning Kulick and his ludicrously curled-up lips to the mercy of the indigenous wildlife and ensuing elements, Skyfire carried her barely burdensome mass across the threshold, absently heeling shut the door. Perhaps an exploit of negligence, permitting a sliver of moonlight to punctuate the ambient glow of his hearth; or a regretful show of assumptive overconfidence that he forewent a more comprehensive security check, and the unhitched door went unnoticed. As he gently fed the enfeebled figure of Kent Pepper into the arms of his great chair, said breach allowed only the passage of cool, crisp coastal nose.

Pepper stirred, her eyes flickering open; at first registering alarm and then a deep resignation as the burdensome reality of the night's horrors robbed her of all vitality and zeal.

"You're safe," Skyfire assured her "Here, drink this. It's only water."

Accepting his glass with trembling hands, she wetted her cracked and downcast lips as a gesture of humility and gratitude.

"I'll telephone the police as soon as you think you're ready." he said. "Who was that chasing you?"

"I don't even know," Pepper sobbed. "*My Dad*. I think they killed *my dad*. They cut him all up."

"There were more of 'em?" Skyfire wanted to know.

"I think there were three, but one of them was shot," she said. "I shot the girl myself, then I ran."

"A girl?" asked Skyfire, shocked. "A girl was involved in all this?"

"If what I saw was any indication, she was the worst." Pepper warbled. "I never saw anything like it."

"Where in the blue *fuck* did this world get so mean?" Nicky shook his head in bemusement.

"Can we go check on my dad?" she pleaded. "Maybe he's still alive!"

"I'd strongly suggest you leave that to the police. Do you feel like you're ready to talk to 'em?"

"What choice do I have?" Pepper asked weakly. "Hey. Thanks, mister."

A foil to the natural majesty of Len colliery, a poisonous lizard born of man crept 'neath the cleansing moon; such divine might as to buckle oceans, yet this contemptible speck trod, filled with an abiding vehemence no lunar influence would sway.

An irascible blight on those whose lives we visited in so far as this tale winds, and indicative of a dark and inexorable pull from below the desolate riverside coals where none cared dig.

Nary a chance had stood this spoiler of innocents and of beneficiaries, quester of the ruin of such that she'd been denied, torn from her still-forming body like a soul, and leaving behind a jewel; flawed, as an egg cracked of haste should render spastic young.

Death hung about like a pestilent halo that swarmed of the bowed cripple, but not so much an affiliate, for its darkly ethereal hooks were a crutch for her borrowed steps.

And in the end, all men are felled with the same methodical belligerence.

This reptile crept 'neath a lamenting moon, its silver tears lighting the way.

"Kid" Nicky Skyfire jabbed at the dial of his vintage rotary telephone as Kent shakily fingered her liberated Derringer through the lining of her jacket. She absently listened as he huffed and boomed a concise and succinct exchange through the ample thatch of his strongman's moustache, before returning the receiver to its cradle and giving her his full attention such as her father had always done, neither party aware of the interstice through which a light fog yawned. Moonlit clouds sailed silently by Skyfire's porch, their luminescent urgencies pressing not one whit upon the concerns of those awaiting the intervention of emergency services in this short series of tragically violent and unlawful events.

"You've no idea who any of these shitstains were?" Nicky enquired of Kent.

"No way," she answered. "I never saw any of 'em before."

"You'd think we'd be safe out here in the perimeter," Nicky went on. "That it'd be too much effort for the *fucking* mouth breathers to hike out here and wheeze on a good folks' program."

In stark, manifest contradiction to his projection, from the darting shadows cast by his open fire, there promptly loomed a guileful black garb from which flickered a long and jagged claw, chewing deeply and audibly into the crook of his neck with a spray of blood and a begrudging hiss like the tearing of an orange.

"*Up* your *fucking* program," rasped the bedraggled mask of Lynette Hunter, maximising the damage inflicted by her inured weapon with a twist and a whisk of her bloodied hands. Despite being shot, this beautiful hound had hauled her wearied bones across the slip of wasteland 'twixt the Skyfire and Pepper properties to exact a poorly justified revenge for the termination of her luckless crew. As the previously unrivalled strength waned from Kid Nicky's bleeding body and he tipped to the floor in an undignified pile of unmerited murder happed up in resilient cotton, Hunter faced off against the sweetly blessed Kent Pepper; a fistful of golden rings versus a crudely homespun tattoo that read *heroin is here for the shitheads*.

"Get up, you uncle-fucking cunt," Hunter gestured with her knife, and regardless of her endless cascade of hopelessly embedded issues and complexities she was a manifestation of devastating attraction, having the world's supply of sex appeal, notwithstanding her tangled, sweaty, and piss-soaked undercarriage.

Just then there came a clap, a jolting peal of thunder, as though a strong and tough paper bag had been promptly burst. Hunter's head, all red lips and pretty lashes bobbed rhythmically, her mouth agape like a tilted crescent moon, until eventually her knees buckled and she dropped over dead in a malodorous hillock of spent venom, and from an irregular protrusion within the folds of Kent's tracksuit jacket curled a grey spook of pungent smoke, and there burned a neat, fiery ring.

At this juncture, what else remained for Kent Pepper but to assume that everyone was dead; to await medical assistance and presumably some cursory form of crisis counselling?

Her eyes glazed, adopting the domestic equivalent of the *thousand-yard stare*, a characteristic of post-traumatic stress disorder usually associated with battle-weary soldiers; and as her quarry's squandered life ebbed from a hole in her forehead, who's around to say that she wasn't?

Look at Your Game

(The Conjected Inauguration of Animal Strap)

This girl, Melanie Lipton? Well, not to get all forthright and overtly masculine, and me being disinclined to appease my inflated sense of self-worth, but I was pumping it right in her face pretty hard and her godawful *c-jet* teeth kept chafing me, which brought very little to the table with regards to me *approaching the Billy Mill Roundabout* (and that's a local euphemism for reaching the hallowed peak of male sexual climax).

My name is Skeeter Young, and I play guitar. I'll never be a virtuoso or anything close to that, but I can string a few chords together and throw in enough *pull-offs* to wow those girls in the front row, whose combined experience of musicianship was that time I made the dark one's little sister in the toilets of a venue that doesn't exist anymore. That slip of the tongue aside, I play lead guitar in a band called Animal Strap with four other guys. The whole world is an ashtray now, and unless you're in a band or a street gang, the likelihood is you'll barely even register on any kind of social scale; but then a lot of folks don't wanna, and I can totally empathise with that. In these days of almost complete lawlessness, the only means of survival for some is to burrow and blag, scavenge and drag, it just ain't for me.

Consequently, I was imposing on this *harridan's* hospitality after a show, with my dick in her mouth and her husband was presumably asleep at the opposite end of the shack. I'd no genuine malaise other than I couldn't come due to the quantities of liquor we'd enjoyed, and the whole scene was developing a somewhat bitter and bogus ambience. In a moment of misappropriated liberty, I reached between her splayed and doughy legs and inside her red satin panties with black lace trim as she continued to *teethe* on my penis. Furrowing my way through the hot coil of pubic hair that furnished her sucking hole, I slid my index finger into her anus, entirely without forewarning or ceremony. Well, this Lipton chick just went bananas, like I'd rigged her up to a defibrillator or something. The way she bucked and convulsed with her mouth full, anyone would think lewd snapshots of her children had just tipped out of my wallet, and there's me just trying to be sensually adventurous within a mutually advantageous structure.

At this stage you'd be forgiven for thinking that the scene was pretty much concluded, and that gracefully cutting our losses would be the logical closure point for myself and the selectively conservative Melanie Lipton, and that was right when her frugal bed collapsed underneath us.

Now Melanie wasn't a heifer by any means, but then she wasn't exactly built for the physical adversities of long distance running either, so when that tin-pot piece of fibreboard horseshit fell apart below our struggling masses, it did so with great aplomb and wanted everyone to know about it. As luck would have it, I negotiated this obstacle unscathed, besides the superficial damage to my dignity due to being pinned beneath my latterly unwilling partner in a state of semi-undress. This was unfolding as one of those cautionary tales that you only ever imparted within a competitive context, and under conditions of collective inebriation; that is, if you allowed sufficient passage of time to erode the salty sting of humiliation and embitterment.

Electing that it was time to vacate this shitshow before the furious intervention of an emblematic husband from the sour depths of Hicksville, Desolation, pop. four, I disentangled myself and eloped through the tiny bedroom window, consequently gouging my narrow flank on the threaded window peg. Once outside the dilapidated chalet I was easily able to disassociate from these recent horrors and consider my next liability, having taken the jocular opportunity to sniff my finger in a moment of laddish indulgence, savouring the surprisingly palatable and arousing fragrance of *trailer musk*.

Outside the little tenement of Boing Court life continued in subnormal fashion; rain fell and litter blew, braziers burned, and fortune favoured few. Later that day I had a band rehearsal to attend, provided our Colin wasn't currently indulging any catastrophic issues in any aspect of his life, as such was his wont. His recent paranoid delusions included the total destruction of his electric mobile telephone, as he maintained it to be a hazardous and clandestine conduit for interdimensional expedition; and in addition to his recurring psychological meltdowns there was the ever-present frailty of the ineptly converted minibus that he used to ferry our beloved equipment. At this point it would be commendable to offer some manner of integral redemption for the sadly afflicted Colin Gash, but in fact he was just a fat, sweaty dick.

A testimony to the devolution of these grave times, there stood a man in curious collaboration with an oddly malformed gargoyle of a boy as I walked across the square, my motives and meditations my own. As the man sang in accompaniment to an admirably rhythmic gyration of his hips and a pantomime-standard handclap, his palsied little charge shuffled a somewhat poignant jig, seemingly hampered by the limitations of its irregular limbs, and although its handicaps included a hairy face and horns, it appeared jubilant. Doubtless contenders for the regard of such coveted entertainment hotspots as those frequented by yours truly and Animal Strap, I worried for the dizzying potential of *One Man and his Dancing Humanoid Goat*, although in hindsight, the singer exhibited all the hallmarks of a nauseatingly foppish cunt as well. Fuck them, and their skewed perception of originality.

Leaving the square and all the whimsical fancies of the peculiar duo, I was jarred from my thoughts by the blatting of a car horn from the road running adjacent to nearby Maddison Street, and was delighted by the definitive face of rock and roll beheld by the rugged old trooper, Tripper Treadmore. Relieved to have been ventured an opportunity to quickly dispense with this ghastly landscape and its chambers of horror, including any further intrusions at the hands of the lustful Melanie or the fiendish little stripe of shit still cavorting with his sissy principal, I practically dove into his archaic shell of a vehicle.

"Hey, what's goin' on?" enquired Treadmore excitedly, holding out his great, bony bear paw for a welcoming high five as I dug my legs into the protesting accumulation of garbage in the passenger footwell.

"Ain't a damn thing changed, man," I answered, keen to be home, to be warmed by the soothing lick of my own bed linen.

"You only just heading on home now? Where've you been until now?" he wanted to know. "Oh, man, don't tell me. I can fill in the blank spaces. You stink like an old lady's glandular secretions."

"Guilty," I admitted. "And how unsurprisingly astute of you."

"You're a love machine," he jibed. "You're gonna have my automobile smelling like a stay-at-home mummy's laundry pile the day after payday."

I laughed heartily despite my mounting fatigue, my fingers pressed lightly on the window glass. I watched as a host of ugly grey clouds peppered their acidic loads onto the dull, Autumnal landscape, supplementing the hostile urban lakes that would never bear fruit, but could only serve as a burden to the lowly pedestrian and an opportunistic snare for silt-beladen snack wrappers; worlds within worlds, if you will.

Ascertaining that I was indeed a spent force and would entertain no further temptations of nasty contraband such as the sour crystalline froth that kept Tripper's motor runnin', or even the cool solace of a free glass of beer, I was delivered to my door; my scabbed and weather-beaten portal beyond which I was able to immerse myself in the reassuring and regenerative pool of my own self-destructive id. Curtains closed against the withering glare of this grey daylight and all its debilitating judgement, I buried my head in shadow and willed that oblivion take my whirling cognizance, were it not for my dirty finger and Melanie's lingering taint lighting an unwelcome fire in my belly.

Oh, beautiful, rose-tinted morning. You positively *reek* of potential, your soft pillars of brilliance aflame amid my thick and whirling dusts. How your splendour buoys me from a lifetime of doldrums, and of submitting to the pitfalls abound these dark and savage days. How your persistence shines eternal, rolling always like unstoppable thunder, impartial of the ways of man, for he is but a chapter to be descried.

Now this date had all the integral ingredients to be among the most epic in recent memory. Still sailing high on the seas of arrogant vice following last night's debacle of debauchery, I considered the day's itinerary, as such was my daily pleasure before departing my comfortable nest and assuming my position in this macabre and irreversibly altered rat race. It was a period of diurnal reflection during which I was of my most balmy disposition; naked and outlawed, I drew my plans against the foe.

That night, Animal Strap were booked to play to a baying crowd at The Odyssey, for all intents and purposes an uninspiring dive, and often the subject of grave and disapproving gossip comprised of sensationalised tales of violent disturbances, rape and in one instance, manslaughter. On this occasion, however, it was rumoured that whatever passed for talent scouts in this bleak, forsaken age was most definitely in attendance. A lucky break for the dead-end sentinels of acid rock and roll could have presented us with tickets out of the metaphorical whirlpool of urban blight, or at least have bestowed us with a rudimentary floatation device long enough to get a foothold towards some other fabulous disaster. Failing that, we were still poised to tear that fucking place up, laying down some purely bitchin' raw power and attitude to make the children of tomorrow raise their hands when they understand. Then, when the music was over, we'd really let loose in the sordid underbelly of rock's last church, taking full and exploitive advantage of the late liquor license and affable junkies, and in all likelihood there'd be another Melanie, maybe even without such an aversion to rectal exploration and the gentle wonderment thereof. With goals like those, who needed structure and stability?

In an effort to dispel the cursory infirmities brought about by last night's excesses, I followed my conditional route to recovery by sealing myself away from detrimental interferences such as noise, daylight, and human interaction, filling my desiccated cheeks with such nourishing fancies as leftover pizza and potato chip sandwiches. Between snacks, I attempted to stimulate my flagging brain by playing video games for extended periods, breaking only to urinate under duress. The sheer addictiveness and robust appeal of the highly successful Man-Made Mudman series was sufficient to whet my appetite for gleeful abandon and distract me from the fantods of a chemical comedown for the entire afternoon; in fact, so overwhelming was its allure that I skirted within a *fanny's hair* of foregoing our critically important show in favour of garnering another handful of jingling gold rings at the hands of that bouncing brown son of a bitch.

Ultimately, it would be scarcely worth the physical beating and subsequent shunning I'd endure at the hands of Colin and the rest of the band upon my absence, and despite my poor mental and physical condition at present, I had sense to determine that I was a massive arsehole for even entertaining the notion of rebuffing my public. What possible grounds existed under which I could justify the selfish containment of this outrageous and electric rock and roll animal?

Shutting down my humbled console, it was with measured regret that I renounced that dope-ass mudman and turned my full attention to this century's holy grail of musical instruments, my snow-white Buxton G B custom electric guitar with gold hardware. A desirable piece of kit during the period of its production, to an attentive collector in these protean times it could certainly be valued above the sterling merit of my scrawny neck. I stowed it carefully in its bulky black hard case, emblazoned with the white-painted legend SKEETER; a legend indeed. It was time to go to work. This wasn't any old bullshit corporate picnic. This was rock and roll.

Having picked my way through battle-torn streets to the burned-out ruin of Chris the cat's former garage where I was scheduled for pickup, I took up what I'd hoped would be a short vigil beneath a jagged outcrop of crumbling masonry, piping on a fat stogie as a fence against the damp cold. Whatever happened to the genial old Chris was anyone's guess, pertinent rumours these days were like currency. If someone imparted a squat, gleaming nugget of information it was like being handed a batch of fresh fruit or other such luxury item, and you ran to trade it for something else. Some say he perished in the wild seas of 'Mare after being bewitched, while others claim he was burned alive in the cinders of a collapsed cathedral. If I may be permitted a moment of brutal honesty as the wind howls through the frayed apertures in my aged denim, chilling my diminishing gems and pebbling my flesh, I gave less than a shiny shite for the fate of Chris the cat. So far as I was aware, the cat had been diagnosed as being crazier than a shot at rat, and besides the wreckage of his tin-pot garage keeping the rain off me, had precious little bearing on my immediate predicament or the whereabouts of his loony counterpart, the elusive Colin Gash.

Tested beyond all reasonable expectations, in an episode of uncharacteristic clarity I recalled both the stock of my blue zippy pencil case, and its relevance in this dire quandary. A quirky relic from my adolescent schooldays, the blue pencil case with a temperamental zip was tagged with the guys' names and telephone numbers, and in case of emergency was secreted in the jetted pocket of my threadbare denim coat. Considering his relevant psychotic episode, Colin's number was now obsolete, but there was a fair to middling possibility that one of the more fastidious members of Animal Strap would respond to my dilemma; and so I drew my *krelboyne* stationary into the glow provided by the lamps in what remained of the garage forecourt. To my dismay, the amber radiance that fell about my shoulders served only to merge the fluorescent pink characters described on the vinyl pouch, rendering them illegible, and to further compound my struggle, the fine accursed rain was sufficient to dilute them to the consistency of neon tears. These were grave times indeed, and thus perilous circumstances warranted immediate and decisive actions. Such was the depth of my conviction and dedication to the continued growth of the shock rock movement spearheaded by the purely sexual big cats of heavy metal, Animal Strap.

Snatching my guitar case from the reflective grit and slurry of the forecourt, I made off into the night, hopelessly optimistic that some kindly and aspiring neighbour would assist me along the way, ferrying my damp ass to the far-flung Odyssey before such a time that the whole situation would be deemed irreparable. If it weren't for the footling prospect offered by Animal Strap, then what the hell else would I do with my worthless existence? These days if you weren't in a band or able to depend upon the abetment offered by your street-gang brothers, then you weren't nuthin'; and would be casually regarded as such.

I picked my way through a concrete maze of aggressively jagged twists and turns, sinister gangland tags and grime-spotted homespun flags, my hand fast on the black handle of my prized Buxton hard case. Corroded and crudely customized vehicles growled by discharging a hostile fog of choking exhaust, their passengers curious and greedy, faces aglow with pent up frustration and rage for a world that had failed them. With no amenable target for their collective despondencies, where were they to direct their fields of regret, besides that which they covet? I darted, slipped, and tripped amid the bloodstained parish, sodden with the sky's caustic deluge and afraid for my life, labouring under the faltering conviction that I would soon emerge within a gentle walk of The Odyssey's colossal stone towers and be incited to fall into a musical nightmare, the likes of which would shackle my heart and commandeer my brain with the promise of tease and sleaze. So delicious and affecting were these tantalising favours that I was loathe to acknowledge the fading recognition of my surroundings. Though it chilled me to admit, the unthinkable had happened and I was lost. So close to home, yet unfamiliar with this challenging landscape and its ever-changing facets; so absorbed had I been with terrors of the dark that I'd wandered, wandered as a panicked lamb, my struggled throes working me deeper into a primordial swamp from which my bones would be picked by a furtling, investigative hand long after my piddling, trivial legacy had been forgotten and my possessions were nought but an insight into *the way it used to be.*

Galled by the dripping of rainwater into my eyes and its subsequent carriage of stinging purple hairspray from my now floundering crest, I ducked into the remains of a once-gleaming erection, two storeys of dereliction and evaporated prosperity crumbling above me. Suffice that these skeletal remains of commerce kept the rain from my back and permitted me sanctuary that I might find my bearings, although the issue of that luxury was now compounded thanks to the recent demolition of the Remco chimneys that had dominated the town skyline for as long as most could remember. For decades those twin throats had been piping great prodigious clouds of noxious death into the atmosphere, their illuminations correcting many a wayward son of his passage home across the years, filled with the spoils of a week's labour spent down The Fleece with the unclean denizens of debauchery and dishonesty. So feared and renowned were The Fleece's mildewed portals, it was widely believed that therein laboured a sag-tit, wire-haired and toothless old redhead barmaid named Bella, that could halve an apple with her bare hands as easy as falling off a log. But I digress; it was my understanding at this juncture that I was close to the concrete shell of old Peter the barber's shop, and that there existed within reach a subway that would lead me right to the perimeter of The Odyssey's ample car park. Pertinent yet, that I should harken to old Peter and The Fleece in such fluid succession, as the icy grip beheld by its demon hooch had been integral in the fall of his barbering aspirations, leaving only memories of his tapping comb and some smashed tiles to his credit.

As nimbly as I dared, I forewent the shelter provided by the leaning masonry, flaking tangles of rebar and clumps of cheesy plaster to brave the perils of the pissy underpass. Spurning my fond remembrances I dove into the street, and the blustering mist driven on by hell's gales. Never a choice thoroughfare, the subway's terrible yawing maw was a discouraging spectacle, exacerbated by the ever-present tide of urine that layered its nethermost station and contributed most of its reek, periodically supplemented by dead pets and random snarls of upholstery. A ribbon of decaying lights bathed the entire rotten tube in a jaundiced milk, floodlighting the rarely articulate graffiti and encouraging safe passage for those opposed to jaywalking across the flyover. All things considered, the expedience proffered by the revolting underpass carried little weight against the demoralising traumas one could conceivably sustain as a result of riding it.

Despite my innumerable reservations I plunged into the abyss of piss, making satisfactory progress whilst performing an unusual and unflattering prance in avoidance of the many unhygienic hazards peppering the skin of rancid silt.

Great fissures gaped in eternal woe from the subway's tiled walls, expansive and astonishingly deep craters that hooked and wound deep into the surrounding earth and shone with eerie, flickering light. What manner of poor and desperate vagrants should be compelled to scrape and cleave of this rotten crevasse to fashion a rudimentary network of galleries in proximity to dire squalor of such measurement? My empathic considerations were ceased with shrill and sudden punch as a menacing procession of humanoid silhouettes hove into view, their stark, hooded figures highlighted by the glare from the opposite end of the tunnel; that which would have delivered me unto safe and glad occasion. And to think of the countless hours spent ogling clichéd horror movies warning us of the jeopardy surrounding such bleak and unsecured locations; particularly those with dramatic lighting effects and howling winds, endless dripping of foul, echoing waters and discarded plush toys with one shiny eye and a burst sphincter. The deliberately obstructive stance that these obvious delinquents had adopted was indicative of their malicious intent towards my trespass, and due to the encumbrance of my vintage heavy metal munitions, retracing my steps would be an entirely abortive exercise. I'd be captured long before I reached the subway entrance to make good my escape.

Slowly, inexorably, the dark hoodlums advanced upon my position, presenting me with three options, as I saw it. If I was to ditch the Buxton G B, leaving what was in all probability the last of its kind to the mercy of these loathsome scavengers, then I projected my chances of a successful dodge. Alas, I would no more abandon my miracle of rock and roll evolution to this shower of dirty, knuckle-dragging reprobates than I would bid them partake of my mother's fancies; rather that I should fight them tooth and nail, suffering a hero's fate than to conceive of their sooty sausage fingers manhandling my tremolo arm with a preposterous lack of grace. In stark, abject clarity, so I beheld a most insipid choice, and was directly supplemented with a third recourse as I hearkened to the clawed fissures in which there winked a troubled candlelight and the beguiling opportunity of freedom.

It was my opinion that to engage this party of rude and subnormal primates in a good old-fashioned *scrap* would inevitably result in them usurping my precious guitar anyway, and so I body-swerved into the nearest craggy rift and had away into the murk.

With no knowledge of what possible cancers lay ahead, I sidestepped and cantered through the chaotic debris, my beloved Buxton hard case shipping many a clip and a bump as I negotiated the irregular stone capillaries to show my antagonists a clean pair of heels. Within a very short spell, and to my overwhelming relief I was able to relish a fresh and invigorating wind about my cheeks and quickened my pace forthwith, eschewing the clusters of empty cans and bottles that rang with every footstep, and jagged spires of masonry that threatened to brain me in the twilight dim.

Relenting to the sterile glare of fluorescent lighting, the passage eventually opened onto a basement of sorts; all drooping copper pipes, kinked and laden about with spongy scoops of sodden, mildewed plaster amid household debris and battered doors hung askew. Aspiring to gain the higher ground I scrambled atop heaps of demolition rubble, yet my frenzied motions succeeded only in displacing the higgledy-piggledy formations of flotsam, and as I cast a despairing eye about this crumbled pile, I caught sight of a face filled with malicious spite. So it came to pass that my flight hadn't been quite so fluid as I'd hoped, and my would-be captors had all but cornered their quarry in this putrid corner of scorched earth. Their big-eared coupons positively radiated unwarranted loathing, and it fairly curdled my racing blood to behold such an empty and indomitable fearlessness in the eyes of those so scarcely evolved from infancy. Essentially waylaid, I had little remaining option but to fight, and as one particularly rat-faced and barefoot little runt shaped up to me in this moss-dappled arena, I grudgingly relinquished the Buxton G B and steeled myself to bang heads against the foe.

Though I'm reluctant to admit, I shipped a brief and wry admiration for this gutsy character in his initiative, although despite his fervour and venomous pep I was quickly able to gain the upper hand; being of the rather desperate standpoint that having made an example of the little shit, his reptile cohorts would slither back into whatever sordid grief-hole from whence they'd come. Clamping my adrenaline-fortified mitt around his neck I was easily able to pivot him, eventually driving his repulsive mask into a supporting wall, thus engaging a damage multiplier the likes of which a drywall counterpart would've been found wanting. Not to glorify this sadly requisite slaying, but with every successive blow there was an increasingly gratifying splash of claret, and the accompanying gnash of splintered bone until eventually the wretched, bottom-feeding parasite fell limp in my kindled grip and his thrift-shop trousers became awash with pee. Nevertheless intent on breaking the will of these jobsworth pirates, I succumbed to a final squeeze of his faggot choirboy wig, likely tearing of my own distended muscle in the effort of coaxing another tooth or even a haemorrhaged eye from his pathetic, lifeless dome.

I allowed his carcass to fall; one with the other bygone reveries here in copious superabundance. Snatching my guitar case from the gritty slough I made off into the sleet, no longer concerned with unrealistic dreams of rock superstardom, but more preoccupied with the security, familiarity, and relative warmth of my home.

Emerging from that infernal basement, I left the remaining maggots to huddle about their fallen brother, no doubt to cradle his sweet, misunderstood melon, and to petition the Lord as to what possible justification existed to warrant such cold injustice in these times. I thence found myself within the asphalt geometry of a quadrangle like that in which I'd previously witnessed the odd partnership of man and malodorous bugbear upon my departure from Melanie's nest; although this court sparked little resonance with me. Seemingly oblivious to the appalling weather, a group of lithe and sinewy men in gangland colours were alerted to my advent, and crowded me accordingly, their vests divulging them to be an indigenous branch of THE FLAILS. Upon initial contact, an apparently non-violent assemblage; their clothing displayed images of fairies and such truck, and my battle-damaged hard case had sparked keen interest among their numbers.

Fuck Colin Gash, I thought to myself.

Rue de la Châtaigne

(The Loss of Innocence)

Deep down inside, though I hadn't been within a stone's throw of Rue de la Châtiagne in more years than I cared to remember, I knew that on fastening my weary eyes upon that strangely flat-topped box of a house that I'd be practically poleaxed by an overwhelming rush of bittersweet memories and buried emotions. This was an ugly neighbourhood and always had been, but to a child of the tender age such as I'd been when our tiny family expanded to fill out the woodchip rooms of number one hundred, maudlin issues like those pertain to the adult world and go largely unnoticed. In all honesty, stood here in the shit-pocked fields opposite my revered childhood home, swathed in a cotton tracksuit and fast approaching fifty, I'd have been a lot more comfortable mounted on the saddle of a competitive bicycle than reliant on the tenacity of my old bones to propel me out of danger in this neck of the woods.

Things had certainly changed since my last tenure, although not so fundamentally. Efforts had been made towards improving the general standards of living throughout these blood-soaked twists and turns, but low-quality residences they would remain; this entire district could be likened to a gigantic bowel. In their efforts to inject values and respectability into the area, the local committees had merely stripped away some of the dusty sugar coating that had formed many of my reminiscences and fondly poignant scars. An unexpected and sustained airstrike couldn't cleanse these streets; the soil was bitter.

Where once had lain a wild, sprawling field as seen by the eyes of babies, its limits uncertain and bounties unlimited, there now boasted a neatly clipped and featureless expanse of grass. Cloven in twain by an equally bland path, it now bore the incidental register of error; the walkway a prodigious score as would invalidate an unsatisfactory passage of text. *The tip*, as said field had been unfondly dubbed in our days of virtue, had been a wild and unkempt daily adventure for those arguably unfortunate to have been conceived before the advent of electric video games and the dangerous and blasphemous freedom of the information superhighway. A hotspot for fly-tippers and a temporary retreat for those seeking to escape the social and financial blight of 1980 via means of solvent abuse, the tip nevertheless provided yours truly with an ever-changing landscape filled with natural riches, and an avenue that the inquisitive and imaginative minds of children might flourish in exploration.

Though the tip held its fair share of unsavoury recollections, it was with a grateful appreciation that I was able to fetch its merits to mind and relive those days of jolly freedom, and a wealth of seemingly trivial experiences that would subtly and silently shape me into the only adult male capable of telling this story. Whether the tale contains any practical value or moral enlightenment is thoroughly subjective and remains to be seen, but to me it's cathartic and represents a partial jettison of the self-destructive emotional freight that would bring about the inevitable and lamentable hardening of a young man's soft heart.

Many local features endured, such as I was able to observe in the fleeting spell during which I endeavoured to remain respectfully anonymous and beware of unsettling the paranoid natives, lest they become agitated and unleash hell in the baroque form of their dangerously interbred canine nightmares. The gently winding road along which I'd whiled away endless minutes attempting to become proficient on my battered green skateboard despite challenging impediments of broken glass and coarse aggregate remained intact, eventually relenting to the much larger and woefully unforgiving *pit road*. Although comparatively peaceful in recent times, the pit road's cracked and pitted surface belied a legacy of brutality that could yet stimulate a deep-seated terror by means of the rude introduction of a juvenile mind to a most unwelcome depth of experience. Though I'd warmly likened a precarious proximity to the great, blackened coal lorries that had once dominated this thoroughfare to the terrifyingly rambunctious din of a very specific starship in a series of cinematic productions I adored, they were death on wheels. Indeed, they were instrumental in tearing down the fledgling foundations of a good-natured and amiable station, and giving rise to some darkly subsidiary version of what I could have been; but I'll elucidate further along the way.

One other thing notably absent from this modern-dilapidated wonderland was the string of brick sheds that had previously provided each residence with a pair of lockable outhouses, that the good folk might furnish themselves with horticultural tack to better maintain their council lawns whilst also sustaining a safe and dry cache of coal to warm their kin.

As a youngster I'd dug the occasional duty of collecting fuel for the open fire, as it became something of a personal test of strength to evaluate how comfortably I could wield the filthy scuttle in correspondence to the ratio of coal. Sweeter still was the purported chore of chopping kindling, as I perceived it to be a most enjoyable and satisfactory labour to split those knotted oddments of timber, and to be permitted approach to a bladed weapon with which I could quite conceivably have lopped off a finger. Dim was the day in which I'd subsequently availed myself of the finer points of deception and the resourceful spinning of yarns, as I'd procured the axe in the interests of my own merriment and was busily bashing something, the specifics of which have evaporated in the passage of years. An enduring detail to supplement this cautionary parable was the presence of the nearby fire hydrant sign over which I'd lavished many a fascinated peer with the key to its technical data. I'd marvelled that the sign's lower digit denoted the distance in feet to the fire hydrant itself, and would gladly impart the benefit of my knowledge by means of a demonstration, culminating in the lifting of the cast cover to reveal woolly clusters of spider eggs which we'd mash with sticks. It was, in all probability, the hydrant sign I was bashing, to dislodge the metallic yellow plate with contrasting black *H* as some form of anarchic and rudimentary trophy; it could therefore be construed that I was fairly deserving of my impending casualty. Whilst swinging the stubby axe with gleeful abandon, I'd become suddenly aware of a notable change in its mass, as if the very thing had been robbed from my grasp, yet its roughly splintered haft remained clenched in my grubby fist. Thence, the world faded dark for a time, and I was stricken with a bitter taste in my mouth, though no such lozenge had affected it, and a surprising smart belted throughout my dome. In a most unlikely sequence of trivial tragedies the iron blade had worked itself loose and had sailed in a vertical arc as I readied myself for another swing. Then, the gravitational pull of our sweet mother earth had smote its spiteful clump of metal hostility on top of my bonce, fetching open a gash sufficient that my shaking, exploratory fingers dared touch only once. Torn between the hurried fabrication of a parentally acceptable claim and the explosive release of my pre-pubescent tears, I stashed the traitor axe and concocted a scenario in which I'd been bent double, engaged in the observation of ants, and upon righting myself had gashed my head upon jagged brickwork. Bereft of guilt, I sought comfort in the arms of my beloved young mother, now dead.

Indeed, all that had dwelled there were now deceased. Everyone, dead; aside with their soured dreams. I had become an embodiment of *the lonely man*, a banner for those committed to wander the sidelines staring earthward, an erroneous ambassador to the conviction of lamentable circumstance. A knapsack on my back, I wandered great stretches of quiet rock and lonesome wood to the tune of a most excruciatingly plaintive ballad. Yet, despite the bleak leanings of this deeply intricate and soulfully remorseful picture I've painted, there had transpired many moments of great joy at one hundred Rue de la Châtaigne, or else I shouldn't have returned to rekindle them. The purity of a glee is boosted tenfold when woven alongside woe in a far-reaching tapestry of relentless suffering and dolour. Our penance within that rude mockery of a home read like a children's concise encyclopaedia of death, as such were my stark and punishing introductions to the repulsive, inexorable finality of doom.

My pet rabbit died first. Sniffer, upon whom I'd initially lavished a great deal of wide-eyed affection, but in all probability neglected in favour of my great chaotic cupboard filled with toys, and the boundless adventure they inspired in my juvenile mind. Despite my myriad distractions, I'd harboured a perfect love for my very first pet, and had choked an abundance of racking sobs over its stiff body, having little previous comprehension of the absolute finality of quietus. At such poignant inductions you're presented a metaphorical and irredeemable permit, the quality of bearing which entitles you to have your heart torn roughly apart at scattered junctures for the remaining term of your natural life, or up to a stage when it comes over stony and unresponsive.

In so far as my heavily repressed recollections extend, little Jed died next, and I do hope I've done the poor puppy the respectful service of assigning him his correct title, as these hazy purgatories are many and jumbled. Having only lived a minute of his life, there he was spinning, spinning, his adorable legs collapsing beneath his weight as he appeared to choke on his own regurgitations before falling, panicked and dying. A further scar for the virgin heart, and a repetition of all the accompanying frustrations and crippling, torrid grief. Along the way there lived a big old brute of an Alsatian named Rebel, whom I'd attempted to befriend to assuage the vacuum that existed in place of my own dead pets. A solid playmate, he was nonetheless averse to gestures of affection such as a troubled young boy might be inclined to lavish, and having once embraced his thick neck I was requited with a deep, forewarning growl that fairly put the shits up inside me and sealed the termination of all potential bond. Forty-odd years on, it was an acknowledgeable comfort that the ornery old yellow-toothed bastard would be definitely dead.

Directly opposite my most memorable childhood home there'd churned a dirty great colliery surrounded by spiked metal railings, beyond which a classmate at our local primary school had informed me there were lions. Gifted with an extensive imagination, I remember reasoning that the aforementioned was a plausible claim, as the property extended beyond the scope of my vision and contained considerable scrubland. Afeard to breach colliery security and loathe to incur my wrathful father, I had only to stare and wonder, and became mesmerised by the deep, black wash at the gates permitting passage to the perpetual stream of gargantuan lorries.

A manner of shallow depression was situated just within the aperture allowed by the boundary fence. By all appearances an intentionally man-made feature, it was filled with foul water, blackened by the residual coal dust of dozens of years of shipping *black diamonds* off to those seeking to harness their latent energies. Any and all industrial vehicles affiliated with the transportation of coal had to pass through this trench to conduct their business, and my unworldly logic reasoned that this mandatory function was an automatic wheel washing system. Notwithstanding the absence of any substantial bearing on my overall tale, in light of some cursory research in latter days it transpired that my deductions were correct, and this crude flush was to reduce the carriage of *clarts* onto public highways where they were tied to present a potential menace to other drivers. Lo, it was this rudimentary function that beggared my keen attentions.

Upon ploughing their beastly path through dark waters, the wagons effected a parting of the wavelets during which the base of the trench was tantalisingly visible as the inky mass was repelled on either side. Having occasioned a trough, the aggravated waters would rush back to fill the space, resulting in two opposing tides colliding in the approximate centre, ofttimes with a resounding clap before settling into their former rhythm and shimmer. An easily excitable and gullible child, I was oddly captivated by the near-industrial action of the water and would frequently dart to my window at the noise of a coal truck slowing to enter the gate, watching as the resulting swells slammed into violent coalition, throwing their spume skyward like fleeting diamonds; fallacious and provisional jewels, like each of us. Dark tides closing like the chapters of our lives.

Returning to Rue de la Châtaigne approximately twenty-two years later, I was caught in the seductive thrall of a highly self-destructive phase of life, following the latest in a series of harrowing departures from various romantic interests. Particularly downcast and vulnerable, I sought comfort with the ghosts of my past, as more than any other aspect of my seemingly worthless endeavour they were certain and dependable.

The gate that my spotless and venerated grandfather had installed to restrict the passage of unwelcome mammals into our considerable back garden remained intact, although I doubted its fragile trellis would support my weight as it had done back in 1983. In addition to its badly weathered condition and dashes of colourful lichen, the vines that had once thronged its wooden intricacies were dead and forgotten by all but me. The trellis had permitted access to a latch for those with a groping arm and the relevant direction, that the gate might be opened from outside. The latch had suffered as the vines and only a rust-infused hole remained to betray its existence, although the gate lingered closed as it hung on fucked hinges, swollen with rainwater, and braced against dimpled concrete that put me in mind of either breakfast cereal, spice or ravioli.

The back garden to which I've already alluded was a balding expanse of baked and compacted earth; gone was the tall birdhouse in which nothing ever dwelt, as were the clutch of mint that we'd harvest on Sundays, and the creaking and groaning swing upon which I'd honed my skills as a stuntman and acrobat, and invented the horrid repast of earthworm jerky as the sun beat relentlessly down on brighter days. The colour had drained almost entirely from this dank midden as though fate had confiscated my crayons and ground their jubilance to powder, leaving only a drab vista from which the inexorable passage of daylight cycles was robbing all traces of vibrance and hope. There'd been a decorative tree stump close to the rear windows, under which my parents had secreted a spare key wrapped in plastic, and although the stump around which I'd choreographed my strongman act was gone, presumably rotted away, the starved circle of earth from below its bulk remained a diminishing network of insipid roots and yellowed weed; a dwindling fractal of doomed terrain, over which one could ponder its sad origin.

Second time around at Rue de la Châtaigne, I could've given a fuck for spare keys or their implications with regard to home security. If I remembered to lock *any* of the doors, it was a good day at rock bottom, and although I retained a respectful terror for such mind-altering chemicals as LSD or

MDMA, under the influence of which I could potentially be locked in an abysmally torrid free fall for anything up to fifteen hours, for everything else there was cocaine and speed, or their heavily *bashed* local equivalent, at least. Not to glorify or condone the implementation of recreational drugs, for they could easily have been my undoing, but in the short term they were second to none when applied for the suspension of great, overwhelming hives of first world problems and nagging residual anxieties. For me, the onset of *autonomous sensory meridian response* while I sapped a four-pack of beers and a goodly supply of bitter amphetamines was as close to mother's milk as a grown man could ever get, and right then I needed it.

During my short-term tenancy I availed myself of only the barest essentials in terms of furnishings and creature comforts. My lounge consisted of a burst vinyl couch supplemented by inflatable armchairs and a crooked standard lamp toward which I felt mysterious fondness, and considering the extensive back garden with its formidable walls and fences, I spurned any compulsion towards the purchase of curtains in favour of the al fresco approach. The general attitude of that phase was one of brash indifference, as within a fifty-foot radius there were probably more than a dozen other folk engaged in their own flavour of substance abuse. As fate would have it, their gear was likely a higher grade than mine and should therefore be apprehended first, amid considerable caterwauling and good old conventional roughhousing, of which I could gingerly spectate through my unfettered windows.

My fondly remembered kitchen, in which I'd watched my father gutting worm-laden fish with ardent interest was then a battle-scarred husk of the often-homely hub it had once been. His deft and powerful hands had carved at this repulsive denizen of the sea, irrespective of the curious, threadlike worms until its butchery revealed an almost complete carcass of a shrimp, presumably partially digested, and orange like a carrot. Were it not for the melodramatic, howling protests of my mother at the presence of the abominable marine gargoyle in her kitchen, I'm quite certain it would've eventually graced our plates with a side of new potatoes, hot from a covetous roadside opportunity, and the shrimp would've fed the birds.

Against one wall had stood our dinner table, as so was the manner of those days to tuck such occasional fixtures neatly adjacent to walls. Seated at the table, in my infinite and uncommon curiosity I'd once wondered at the flavour combination of orange juice and buttered bread, and proceeded to sneakily mix the unorthodox paste inside my mouth. By some dreadfully unfavourable twist of fate, perhaps a gag reflex or simply an excess of pressure, my inflamed cheeks involuntarily contracted, unloading my spurious vomit upon the table's polished veneer.

"Have you just been sick?" my mother had blurted, presumably aghast at the unprecedented puddle of masticated sundries I'd presented.

It had been my opinion at that juncture that neither parent would have sympathised with my insatiable interest in the fusion of orange cordial and sliced loaf, and so I'd opted to humour the spew scenario to its fullest. Any further developments to the situation were lost in the annals of time, although I do recall the drop-leaf table operated a most vicious and lethal mechanism, and woe betide any careless manipulation of its stubborn jaws, for it cared little for the agonies of a crushed knuckle or a black man's pinch.

Returning to the issue at hand, engrossed in my destructive bent, so I began a slew of mostly emotionless connections with girls of questionable integrity. I even liked a few of them, although such were their lugubrious upbringings that their characters were largely and irreparably soured, to the extent that I could only pity their feral children and the similar destinies they were doomed to play out. I underwent something of an epiphany on the very evening during which a panicked bantling savage imposed on my recreation in a highly agitated state, having trapped her head in a seaside bucket by means of the plastic handle beneath her chin. Despite my resulting amusement, I was possessed of a profound despair upon watching her inebriate mother negotiate the bright plastic pail with a pair of scissors. Once freed from the bucket, I've no doubt she went on to perform feats of acrobatic distinction whilst swinging from the light flex in her shared bedroom, eventually falling pregnant in her early teens.

Following my modest awakening I began slowly conducting some semblance of a regular life, ditching the harmful narcotics, and eventually moving away from the venomous influence of Rue de la Châtaigne, where it was rare joy to coordinate a conversation without such demoralising terms as *rising damp, leak* and *fungus*. During the emancipation I was able to improve my career prospects, and although I maintained a steady flow of ladies with questionable virtue, theirs were a negligibly higher grade of social standing than the gap-toothed, pallid and bloated *trolley-pigs* with whom I'd formerly held acquaintance. Upon reflection, it was indeed a wonder that I'd come back to replay these jaded clips of a paradise lost, yet faced with dim and gurgling death, a drowning man will clutch at anything to make good his recovery.

Somewhere in the green and golden days of the mid-1980s I'd been idling around the estate, having marvelled at the outlandish behaviour of one friendly dog with which I'd cultivated a tentative bond. I feel it pertinent to add that my classmates were many and varied, but few were local, other than a scattering of rancid stereotypes that always seemed blissfully unaware that they were dangling a retch-inducing milky snot from one nostril. Therefore, I had scant alternative but to carefully seek acquaintance with the indigenous wildlife, most of which were canine. This dog had been worrying at the matured carcass of an anonymous feline, and although its badly eroded body was barely recognisable as a mammal of any denomination, such were the morbidly obsessive natures of children to launch rigorous and probing investigations into the discovery of dead animals, and consequently a cat's face had been positively identified. The sad and atrophied cadaver had covered an impressive distance across the estate, making appearances in various front gardens to eventually find its way into the middle of a road that I've forgotten the name of, presumably as consequence of further ghoulish investigation, and it was there that my doggy companion tumbled it. In addition to a predictable pattern of scratch and sniff, the dog set about rolling around on what was, by this point, a flattened head attached to a flag of stiff hide. It then furthered its routine to include the surprisingly aggressive grinding of its own head into what remained of poor old Jonesy, and despite my resultant gaiety and amusement, became hostile and unapproachable. I marched off indignantly with a final, apologetic glance at the cat's frantic and desperate rictus, and left the wolfish betrayer to its own devices.

Having travelled only a short distance toward the grand old shitshow Châtaigne, I was acknowledged by the comparatively familiar face of a wizened and weather-beaten *Teddy Boy* character toiling at his open garage, and ambled over to investigate. I was relatively sure I'd seen my father conducting amicable exchanges with this cat on several occasions, and therefore wasn't fearful of such dreadful upshots as were commonplace on television news in those days. Public information films shown in schools and cinemas had intended us to be vigilant towards such situations and had a bonus effect of striking a pure and exquisite fear of wolves, shadows, water, caravans and almost the entire general public (particularly men wearing thick glasses), into our vandal hearts. It was difficult to pinpoint, yet some elusive quality to those two-minute slices of blood-curdling terror was sufficient to unsettle the stoutest of bastards and leave an indelible impression on our delicate and sophomoric psyches, upon which one could theorise pertaining to current suicide statistics and subsequent substance addiction, perhaps.

As it transpired, *this* rocker was on the level, and proceeded to awe my impressionable eyes with a big ugly magnet that he held in his possession. Handing me the cold ingot of grey metal, it was as a stage magician permits the audience to inspect his empty top hat, building the suspense upon its disclosure to be entirely free from albino rabbits, doves, or similarly exploitative counterpart. On my obvious confusion at being handed an apparently benign ferrous lump, this Lincoln-looking motherfucker snatched it from my sweating palms and tossed it coolly into the air where it struck the overhead garage door with a rather vexing crash, and to my wonderment, stuck like magic.

"Go on, try and get it," he goaded me.

Arms outstretched, I attempted to retrieve it with thin, scrabbling hands, but was unable to dislodge this evidently powerful Gaussian artefact. As had been the fellow's intention, I was severely impressed, and desired the magnet intensely as I projected my own displays of its uncanny strength in my capacity as schoolyard maverick. Perhaps this old buzzard had discerned my characteristically dishonest intentions, as he retrieved it with a deft and practised twist of his gnarled hand, stowing it on a high shelf beyond reach of my keenly cutpurse fingers before returning to his task of slicing a section of carpet into narrow strips. Further intrigued, I observed his actions awhile before enquiring as to the peculiar mechanics which seemed to concern the detached wheel of a bicycle, its saddle tied up with polythene bags in the manner of devout regulars at the bookmaker.

The man explained with a wily eye, that the long fronds of carpet were an ideal substitute for inflatable rubber inner tubes on his bicycle, and it was at this point that my childish interest waned. In addition to the nagging doubts of a small boy concerning the plausibility of bike tyres filled with inconsistent strips of multi-level loop, I found his overconfidence in his fallacious life-hack disturbing, and if memory serves, I simply made off without another word.

Although it mightn't have occurred on the same day as the rock and roll bicycle farce, fortune conspired against me again, in leading me to what appeared to be the dusty old body of a full-grown rabbit at the foot of the spiked fence surrounding the colliery. A nudge with the toe of my oxblood boot revealed it to be very much alive, and the odd blighter gouged at the pebbly roadside to forge an escape. During the ensuing melee it betrayed its captive status, being secured to the fence via means of a length of string or wire, and in a state of excited bewilderment I rushed off to impart this devilment to my father, as such was my unshakable faith in his resourcefulness.

It turned out that the hapless creature had been ensnared, and after imparting the dynamics of the damnable noose I was left to consider the immeasurable gulf of perception between man and animal, while my father went off to free it. Clearly labouring under the misapprehension that this crippled wild rabbit would be a fitting replacement for Sniffer (deceased), he installed the struggling animal in the vacant hutch amid pride and gloating. Delighted with my new pet, I was crestfallen to learn that it was dead by next morning, and that beyond all reasonable doubt its vain efforts to free itself had mauled its delicate innards sufficient to kill it. As with all previous expiries, I cried a river of the most immaculately authentic sorrow, my mother's encircling arms welcome, but inadequate.

During the short walk from the Ted's garage to my house, I passed the home of a stoic, ageing couple whose names elude me, although it feels appropriate to dub them Sullivans. Ensconced in a house like a wonderful page from modern history, the Sullivans owned an extremely amiable and good-natured Jack Russell terrier named Trixie, with whom I was predictably and fondly acquainted. The couple were similarly affable, and upon Trixie's giving birth to a litter of pups I was permitted to visit awhile as I fancied, and gloried at the basket of stiffly awkward, squeaking little dogs, pink eyes and noses abound. As I sat on the floor, gently stroking the trembling pups, I would gaze about the Sullivan's drawing room, marvelling at the stark contrast to our own, and the neat, wartime flavours to which it clung. While the first lady busied herself with needlepoint or some such girlish endeavour, Mister Sullivan studied a large, upmarket newspaper, his expression stern and authoritative atop the stout magnifying glass with which he navigated its pages. On having assimilated sufficient of their quaint and couthy ambience, I'd quietly and politely announce my desire to leave, and I'd be shown the door, perchance to spend the following evening playing with Trixie, were it not for her haggard condition at being nuzzled and lapped at.

And so it gores at the poorly healed lesions of yesteryear to recount the harrowing passage that will conclude this jumble of woolly memories, for if not, their morals and high points die with me. Talk is cheap, and only in their poetry can these parables be adequately digested.

Having convalesced following the test of motherhood, Trixie bounded throughout the jungle of unchecked hogweed and wild grasses of the tip, a somewhat dumpy gazelle, elated to be companion to myself and the misguided Aldous Sindy who'd joined us for the afternoon. I loved that dog as my own, and irrespective of any incendiary, speculative opinions that may have been formulated due to her unfortunate death, part of my heart was atrophied that day.

Tough as it may be to ween, I genuinely can't recall which of us threw the rubble that Trixie so faithfully chased, radiant and vivacious until her very last moment, although the monumental blunder will be etched in my mind forever. I'll assume the blame, for what it's worth.

The little dog ran to the edge of the wasteland in eager pursuit of the thrown token, oblivious to the smog-belching, heavy metal death engine that had rounded the corner in the form of a thundering coal truck, as the driver was seemingly unaware of our tiny white dog with tan ears and a diamond on her forrid. Despite my warning cries upon the dawning of this fortuitous calamity, Trixie ploughed into the vehicle's wake and lay still, permitting me a moment to beg her salvation as her hindquarters peered at me through the weeds, although it was not to be. Shocked beyond all conceivable doubt, we gingerly assessed the situation to discover that our zestful friend had been blown apart; burst like a dropped fucking watermelon, zero fucks given.

From a respectful distance we watched as Mister Sullivan and a handful of sympathetic neighbours loaded Trixie's remains into a black polythene bag, having confessed our tragedy to my parents. The poor old guy hefted her rear legs into the air that the bag might accept her, eliciting a mournful belch of sobs from his wife as the mangled canopy of blood and flesh was peeled from the loathsome pit road and lowered into the void.

I couldn't tell you why, but at some point, after everyone had returned to their respective homes, presumably to besmirch "those fucking kids" in privacy, Aldous Sindy and I stole our ghoulishly curious way to the spot where little Trixie had met her end, and in addition to the considerable wash of blood, I spotted an intact kidney tucked into the kerb. Upon discovery of the useless, glistening organ, I'd exceeded my maximum capacity of pathos for that day and trudged off home to begin unloading my own intolerable batch of barely comprehensible grief at the mercy of my steadfast and endlessly compassionate mother.

Why then, do I return to this rancorous stretch of soured stone and stained earth?

Throughout life my very meat is woven and spliced with its coarse reminiscence, swaying my every motion like malicious spores, silent and microscopic.

Though I'm carried away as this aged aspect wills it, no joy could unfetter these rusted hooks to which I've grown accustomed, as with a scar or an unseemly ridge of mended bone.

There's a barbed comfort in replaying these remembered matinees.

In teasing at the eschar I can prolong the wound, and thence grace the same pain at my wounded heart's behest.

I still hear the industrial discharge, and I can smell the hogweed.

I still taste exhaust fumes and coal dust, and I feel *everything.*

Layten's Chute

(Those Likely Boys)

Darkly festive glared the cracked and canted stones of Layten's Chute's parish, garish and dissonant in face of those who vainly strove to maintain an iron fist of complete control and forced obedience. Buoyed by one another, this pocket of rebellion revelled in the coloured lights and hot snacks, the shoddy imported merchandise and improvised costumes; corroded relics of what used to be.

Farty speakers dispensed old favourites into the chaotic revelry, supplementing their elation in these snatched episodes of freedom and the fleeting suspension of their miserable dictatorship, and so the custodians among them gazed fondly on their flock with renewed hope.

Far from a small and casual movement, these crippled roads fairly teemed with the defiant masses, an unquiet oppression with an axe to grind for the hopeful ideals of the next generation, if not their own. If not plague that divided this ostensibly useless generation, then bombs and guns herded the human cattle; dogs, chains and fire hoses, riot squads and broken noses. Their sadly hollow palms held only the want for reform and their right to a constitution.

This festival of illuminations and budget fairground attractions was a vital dose of positivity for those present, and a gesture of their indomitable spirit, that despite the government's strong-arm policies they would not be cowed.

Among the revellers, the tall, formidable force of rock and roll's dead history strutted like a metal guru in the form of Mark Gatchman. Excitable and inattentive as a gay infant, and contrary to his brusque demeanour, his sharp eyes were lit by the period novelties and beat-up spacecraft that graced this pocket-sized celebration of existence. Swooping and whirling, those dreadnoughts of television adventure and galactic exploration within the limits of unbridled imagination were patched with reconstituted scrap metal and big licks of reinforced tape, but in the minds of those to whom they were held sovereign; they tore through the infinite blackness of space in search of freedom and the pursuit of honest, wholesome Saturday-night justice.

Close to his tall and well-worn bootheels there ambled two men, who although high-spirited and jovial, fell somewhat short of his extraordinary exuberance and naturally extroverted disposition. Though within Mark Gatchman there beat a good heart of surprising capacity, he was wont to infrequent displays of antisocial and destructive conduct from which he would invariably emerge unscathed and piously nonchalant. Notwithstanding his ofttimes alarming flaws, Mark was a diamond among men, and a considerably gutsy beer-pig.

Though similarly broadsided by the spectacular tin-pot flying machines of the lovingly maintained concessions, Chris "the cat" Harris exhibited a cooler disposition, quaffing appreciatively from his nice-cold, ice-cold beer bottle, and shooting the shit with Neil Foxton. Neil was a proud and patriotic ex-military man, and thereby agonising under an almost constant burden of shame and dissatisfaction at the armed forces' management and imposition of these God-forsaken curfews and boundary restrictions. Since the dissemination of the flesh-curdling virus that had brought the world to its knees and then soundly whipped it on the dick with a thorny bush, great tumultuous divisions had been established, and upheld with lethal force. As many had died in the maintenance of the perfunctory curtailments as had succumbed to the hive-inducing, organ-juicing *whistler*; so-called due to its characteristic quality of eroding the finely delicate skin of one's nose and lips, resulting in a ghastly whistling hiss during respiration. Now something of a torn and regretful maverick, Neil was hopeful of a resolution to these troubled times, that he might look upon his formerly revered figurehead with a measure of respect. Despite being brothers in adversity, Chris Harris wouldn't give a bucket of piss for the monarchy's redemption, regardless of their London heritage. Having forfeit so much to the wretched pandemic, his was a standpoint based on fortune, like a leaf on a breeze.

So genuinely incredible was this unlawful parody of a corporate fair that the unrelated brothers, these conspirators of pleasure, bobbed on the warm tide of positive vibes that a resilient community based on deprivation and constraint had arranged. Shadowed figures ran beneath the coloured beams, like giant opals adorning their ruined clothes and lending them a regal flavour sufficient to commit to their loose leaves of *special times*. Vendors dispensed fragrant meats (although heavily processed and previously unpalatable) like nuggets of divine aspect, slathered with condiments whose aromatic appeal was such to harpoon the senses and water the mouths of babes, giving life to an irascible creature with an appetite so insatiable that one could be tempted to toss the unwary under the bus to squish a breaded sweetmeat between jaws inflamed with fierce hunger. The wild folk thronged, jubilant in their unsanctioned suspension of unpopular convention, and the hive hummed with a collective hope as every man unwittingly lent succour to his nearest brother; so they became as one, a living, breathing muscle of defiance, united in bitter adversity.

Giddy with great cheer and afloat with the heady scents of trampled hay and boiled onions, Neil and Chris shared a story while Mark bounced among the shops and stalls, bent on the acquisition of some tastelessly affordable mass-produced item that would supply a tenuous link to his celebratory past. Chris could have talked underwater, and had a seemingly inexhaustible bank of stories, all in a similar vein of riotously funny bad taste. Farbeit from anyone to suggest they were furnished or manipulated in the interest of a more captivating narrative, but Chris talked shit like a priest, and his gospel rocked a great deal harder than loaves and fishes.

"So there we were in the Youth Association gym, just arsing around because none of us really knew what we were doing," he told Neil. "You know, their equipment was shit, it was like salvage."

"Weren't there any instructors there?" Neil asked.

"Nah, mate," Chris went on. "These local guys couldn't care less, so long as you weren't smashing the centre up or denouncing the church. Besides, they wouldn't have known a bicep curl from foreskin pull-backs. They were just fat, middle-aged guys out to make a few quid and drink free coffee in corduroy trousers."

"Yeah, well," Neil acknowledged. "Carry on."

"Well, there's this big hairy nutcase named Tripper Treadmore," Chris enthused. "He wasn't a bad sort, but just a total maniac, you know? Everywhere he went there was some sort of chaotic fallout. Anyway, a crowd of us was there pumping our amateur iron, and he was in the khazi releasing a chocolate hostage. Next thing we know, he's burst through the door without a stitch of clothing on, and he's still got half a *tod* hangin' out of his arse."

"This really happened?" Neil was sceptical.

"On my honour, guv'nor," said Chris. "He's stood there like a fucking Piltdown Man with his dirty spine poking out, and he thrusts his hands in the air and he just roars."

Neil laughed, the kind of dangerously sincere and unbridled laughter that can seize you by the cuff and momentarily teeter you on the edge of a perilous abyss, at the sump of which there waited lunacy.

"Anyway, he strides across to this barbell and he squats down and smears his shitty backside all along it," Chris continued. "Then he's off back to the toilets to sort 'imself out, and suddenly nobody wants to train anymore."

"I'm guessing that's not the end of this delightful epistle?" asked Neil, having recovered.

"Nah, course not. It gets better," Chris reassured. "So then this total cunt comes in, name of Fenton. Proper sadistic old-school shithouse, and everyone's looking at their shoes hoping he'll pick on someone else and leave them alone. Well, he starts mouthing off about how he could lift more weight than everyone else put together using only his massive hard-on, and he barges in and starts banging out repetitions with the stinky bar. We're all watching and we're fucking terrified in case the penny drops."

As before, Neil was overcome with gales of cognizant laughter. A former soldier, he was no stranger to the kind of depraved practical jokes that involved application of the most basic and repellent human organic functions.

"Just then, Tripper Treadmore comes back from the bog. Well, he ain't scared of nobody, 'cos he's completely fucking barmy and he's about six foot five," Chris explained. "He walks right up to Fenton like all other priorities are rescinded, and he booms *smell your fucking hands!*"

"What happened next?" Neil wanted to know, his smile earnest and generous below watery eyes.

"Nah, that's it done for today, mate," stated Chris. "Always leave 'em wanting more."

"What the devil kind of conclusion was that?" Neil protested. "Whatever happened to Fenton?"

"All in the fullness of time, guv'nor," said Chris. "The real fulfilment isn't in the destination, anyway. It's all about the journey, mate. You just keep on tabbing."

With a wry smile, Neil rolled his tearful eyes and they made off to reconnect with Mark, now spelunking in the frivolously lit souvenir and novelty shops, formerly a damp and webby bend in a strip of fathomless regret and smothered dreams. They found him digging through a wire bucket filled with faded turquoise representations of dinosaurs, warplanes and such, gently shaking every shop-soiled box in wistful reminiscence of his youthful receipt of a model kit with polystyrene cement included. As the tiny plastic parts rattled inside the box, yet firmly attached to annoyingly grabby and spindly *trees*, their soft percussion beat a path across the years to happier times in which the gummy construction of ghouls that cheated death or a celebrated muscle car were among one's only remaining treasures, boastfully untouchable and pristine forever.

The trinket boutique itself was an ailing antique, crisscrossed with oily, sweating beams of timber painted during the rage of an obsolete generation, peddling old-fashioned confectionery favourites like cough candy and rainbow crystals, and everything else coated with a layer of tiny spherical *jimmies*.

"D' you find what you were looking for?" asked Neil.

"I wasn't looking for anything," Mark answered brightly. "Just soaking up the residual energies of all this *amazing* nostalgia before it's completely forgotten and no longer relevant."

"You didn't strike me as the model plane type?" Chris interjected.

"Nah, planes not so much," Mark admitted. "More along the lines of collectible spacecraft and famous monsters."

"You fucking krelboyne," goaded Chris. "Come and 'ave a beer."

"You don't realise how precious this stuff is," said Mark, dropping the model box with an air of nonchalance and simultaneously casting himself as a living oxymoron. "Without our cultural inheritance, what have we got?"

"Modernists is what we have," Neil asserted. "This is, after all, the *modern* world."

"I see," said Mark. "Gone, and she ain't coming back. Tough deal, we ran off the tracks."

The three blithe confederates abandoned the shop in favour of rejoining the seething, rippling swarm of unlawful fun, unified under the grand gesture of nonconformity and wildly flamboyant discontent.

"Holy shit, would you look at that," Mark murmured, suddenly aloof.

Making his way toward a thoroughly spectacular display of lit confections, he was altogether focussed on an object whose mass had been borrowed in an effort to stabilise the towering jars and windowed boxes in the absence of an official risk assessment. With a flagrant, but presumably unintentional disregard for public safety, this skyscraper of winking bulbs and hard-boiled gums clumb way above the heads of the celebrant crowd, asway with the breeze long before the muddled intrusions of Mark Gatchman, bent on the investigation of an outwardly unremarkable white cardboard carton at its base.

"Look, could I just lift these sweetie jars so I can get at this box?" Mark enquired of a bystander, who, in all likelihood, was completely unaffiliated with the precarious stack of stocking-fillers.

Regardless of the would-be vendor's response, Mark's question was largely rhetorical, and he proceeded to jostle the gargantuan sugarload in quest of the box and its subsequent inspection. In his capacity as a hoarder of vintage toys and/or those with a connection to movies and television, he'd spotted what he suspected was the *polar variant* of Man-Made Mudman; celebrated star of the popular video game series, in the exceptionally rare guise of Man-Made Snowman.

"Check this shit out," he shouted happily, excitedly. "You wouldn't *believe* this shit!"

Wrangling with the now-lurching erection of glass-shrouded candies and boxed chocolate, his countenance betrayed the gruff, heavy metal hellion portrayed by his snakeskin boots and hellcat hair, and was softened like a football by the most gleeful and infantile expression, befitting an enraptured tot upon receipt of the first lick from a new puppy. Predictably, as Mark fairly beamed in wondrous appreciation of the untouched resin contours of his collectible action figure, so the hazardous display did eventually exceed its range of reasonable flexibility and unburdened itself about the straw-bedecked tracks. Immediately as the first jar dissolved into a jagged starfield of broken glass and crystallised fruit pips, sirens pealed above the greatest hits of a forgotten era in which it was acceptable to mount a loaded goldfish bowl on your television set; and warning shots gave birth to hysteria.

It seemed that intelligence pertaining to the illicit carnival had been leaked to local authorities who'd responded accordingly, dispatching dozens of beat-up patrol vehicles packed with heavily armed law-enforcement personnel with instructions to diffuse the illuminations and quickly disperse the rebellion via whatever means necessary. Predictably, the unruly human tide fell into a frenzied state of self-preservation, scattering every which way to avoid the advancing conglomerate of helmeted, masked troops sporting big guns and cans of tactical riot-control gas. Men scooped up their children and made for the designated residential areas from whence they'd come, while wives flocked together in screaming, twisting herds of instinctive character. A token fracture group of indignant remonstrators lingered, tearing up bleeding fistfuls of *barney rubble* and cog to throw in an intended hail of bludgeoning death and enfeeblement. Yet, upon deflection of several emblematic chunks of sod and pebble, the enforcers returned fire; having dispensed with their procedural warnings, non-conformists were shorn with bullets and the lanes of Layten's Chute choked with tear gas in a terrifying reprisal of their initially peaceable act of defiance.

A stone's throw from the front line, amid the crackle of glass underfoot (and still in possession of the much sought-after *snowbeast* figurine), Mark and his constant companions fled, knowing all too well that the law-enforcement officers were now shooting to kill, and that in such instances of grand uprising the authorities would be looking to make a violent example of the dissenting proletariat.

"This all feels like your fault, you cunt," said Chris, wheezing.

"I see your point," Mark panted. "But those two events were just an unfortunate coincidence."

"All for that fucking dolly," Chris added. "What is it, anyway?"

"Fucking shut up," Neil remonstrated. "We're heading into a dead end that rests on the border of the desolate."

"Oh, great," said Chris. "I wondered why nobody was following us."

"Then surely this is a shit decision," Mark suggested, slowing. "It's gonna be like shooting fish in a barrel."

"We're gonna have to *make* a way through," said Neil.

"Into the desolate?" Chris yelped.

"It's probably not all it's cracked up to be," Neil joked. "And besides, you're more than welcome to double back and take your chances with the gunners."

"This does seem the lesser of two evils," said Chris, reluctantly.

"S' what, I thought," said Neil.

To the rear, the sharp pop and crackle of gunfire drew ever closer to their precarious advantage, while before them a great boundary loomed, its apex amply laced with barbed wires and threaded with snagged garbage that flapped and tattered like so much faded hope. The imposing walls were peppered with political slogans and vitriolic texts of civil unrest, yet although tall and forbidding, they lacked diligent underpinning and weren't without deficiencies for those with a keen and consistent eye in the face of unwelcome rancour.

"There," Neil snapped, gesturing to a portion of the partitioning wall clad with a most rustic conglomerate of assorted timbers.

There followed a prolonged and desperate cacophony of drumming boots, pounding, and hollering sufficient to arouse suspicion among those of the fascist deployment previously inclined to overlook such a potentially unfavourable impasse. The superficial boards quickly yielded under the flash offensive, relenting to the satisfying crack and splinter of laminated wood, and the reluctant, barking separation of naturally knitted fibres. Fibrous spelks flew like rankled flies, and nails were pulled wailing from their holes as the boys sustained their perilous bid for asylum. As the breach augmented, they delivered their bodies unto its mercy; their flight from the dark into the dank and dismal desolate.

"What the fuck is this, fucking coal?" Chris whined, as he descended an inky embankment, eventually disappearing into a thicket of rushes and tall grass.

"Keep a fucking lid on it," hissed Neil. "We're not out of the woods yet."

"My fucking trousers are filthy," Chris went on.

"I must admit," Mark added. "I've spent better Saturdays."

"Bridge," said Neil. "Just ahead."

Cowering beneath the level of cover afforded by the sparse, yet sickly vegetation, they edged their way to the shadowy sanctuary of the dilapidated railway bridge, while behind them there echoed cries of angered frustration and opportunistic shelling.

"Jesus, they weren't fucking around, were they?" asked Chris, rhetorically. "I shall have to check my pants for little chocolate kisses."

"They won't follow us," said Neil. "But let's not advertise our position just in case one of them fancies 'imself."

Approaching the one-lane bridge, they were met with a massive stone impediment, a gargantuan coagulation of crippled masonry intended to nullify the underpass in its capacity as thoroughfare, although an unladen man with a degree of pluck might easily negotiate its passage under duress. Overhead, stalactites depended from the bridge's filthy underbelly; salty, gritty appendages like tiny condoms dripping with dirty milk. Unwilling to lavish what remained of their precious evening beneath the shelter of this quaint and frugal wonder of civil engineering, the discerning trio made for a nearby row of single-storey houses in which several flickering lights betrayed a suggestion of habitation. Establishing camp and whiling away a balmy evening within the relative comfort of a bivouac fashioned from salvage could be an exhilarating and grounding experience, but while the threat of an ambitious marshal hung like an errant pall of rectal gas in the otherwise crisp and potable air, the boys were concurrent in the decision to flee Layten's troubled borders.

"What is that thing you're carrying, anyway?" asked Neil of Mark.

"It's a souvenir," Mark answered. "A memento of our race with the devil, if you will."

Lilting his eyebrows complacently, Neil led them to the closest house with a glow at the window, rapping lightly at the door in the most routinely patriotic of paradiddles. After a time it was opened by what remained of a human man, and little could have prepared the boys for the ambling shambles that received them kicking their heels in the dark cold, despite having been made aware of the devastating effects of *whistler* since its arrival on their blustery shores several years past. It seemed that their expectations of a life in the desolate had been somewhat sanguine, coloured by heavily improvised tales shared within a sheltered community whose recreational privileges were scant.

They beheld a being whose flesh was comparable to a living carpet of oily peat, yet his eyes, though clearly burdened beyond reasonable human expectations, appeared lucid and wholly coherent. Naked (although within his tarry runnels of collapsing tissue there may well have nestled the decaying memories of finery), his gelatinous penis was diminished to little more than a boastful strand of seaweed and leaked a most frightfully coloured froth of smoking poison. More unsettling than the ghoulish tableau presented by this terrible remnant of a human being was the notorious and ghastly whistling as his devastated lungs wrenched air through apertures clogged with reeking, toxic mucous. Indeed, it would be a wonder if this wretched collection of decayed organs absorbed another sunrise. Pride set these creatures about their daily business, and despite their appalling physical blight, for this they were commendable.

"We're sorry to have bothered you, sir," Neil began, ever the personable spokesman. "But we just broke out of Layten's Chute following some regrettable conflict."

The pinguid man simply stared, as if engaged in some deep and worrisome contemplation.

"We were hoping that perhaps you'd be kind enough to offer some direction?" Neil went on. "I guess that under the circumstances, you could say we're fugitives now."

After an interminable period of wheezing, and an uneasy fluttering at the tendrils of fungal mire that threatened to seal his nasal cavity should they ever be permitted to harden, the man stood back and bade them enter his realm at the obvious risk of contracting his accursed affliction.

"We appreciate this," Neil ventured, recognising the importance of the gesture, should it allow them a moderately broader scope in their grave bid for freedom.

Shuffling over the threshold, they were immediately appreciative of the fire's warm embrace, and though the domicile fairly swam with the malodorous trace of an unsettling and mildewed offensive, they received alms and were keen to heed all counsel. Mark, bringing up the rear with an uncharacteristic clasp of his ham-hands in the relative obscurity of his shadowed posterior, held firm to his hard-won snowbeast. To be sure, this moribund collective offered a share of the chicken trifle they held dear, but to bogart on a man's limited edition action figure in its original box was frankly ludicrous, from a certain point of view.

Their benefactor led them over the dirt floor of his house, which was host to a shower of similar, inquisitive casualties of whistler. The boys were humbled to be in the presence of such a wealth of lingering death, discomfited by their inability to present aid. Though their hearts were strong, beating a surfeit of bright and healthy blood, they could offer nothing but their weak and transitory sympathies, bowing their heads in shame of their functioning bodies as these were regarded with envious eyes.

"I like your shirt," one girl ventured, her tilted countenance fixed on Chris the cat's depiction of a vilified monarch, its eye pierced with a plastic jewel; an unintentional irony concerning what wealth's worth when weighed in context.

"Thanks," Chris offered. "We can swap if you like?"

Abruptly shunted by Mark's burgeoning belly, Chris resumed their caravan of humility as it wound through the unsophisticated dwelling and they were led outside into a great paddock of sorts, its fringes indistinct as they were consumed by the imposing darkness. Pinguid man spake dolorously, in a voice like thunder bubbled through a funnel of thin mud.

"Go straight on," he began, pointing away to the clouded moon. "Right, then left."

At the dropping of the final syllable it was clear that any proceedings the man cared to conduct were concluded, and the boys considered their measures furtively.

"Thank you," said Neil. "You've done us a great service."

Grateful, but nonetheless keen to put miles between themselves and these walking carcasses of men that were outcast in the huge and anarchic emptiness of the desolate, the likely boys made off into the moon's pallid glow, their footfalls dampened by yielding sod. Gnarled and imposing hedgerows on either side supplied a chilling ambience akin to the boundaries of an elaborate gladiatorial arena, in which our three unwitting combatants were coerced into a game of death, such that there could be only one victor against surreal and insurmountable odds. Quickening their pace beneath the stars, they headed for a spot on the horizon that was bathed in a soft amber radiance; and which, on their eventual approach, revealed that within this urban province streetlights still burned. Though the area appeared deserted, it was decreed the syndicate should split in view of their projected odds of survival as individual units, and so they fled, each pursuing their private destiny upon dissension from the indignities of a tyrannised existence in Layten's Chute.

During a bleak and harrowing chore engaged in the primary objective of thriving within this tragic war against the machine, Chris "the cat" Harris learned a great deal about his his own tenacity, whilst frequently pondering the fates of his two estranged chums in their own solitary campaigns. Neil, he was convinced would win out, having been officially trained to adapt and emerge the master of his own balk and misfortune, whereas Mark might falter, having been accustomed to a more privileged heritage. Yet, despite this arguable handicap, Mark was an affable and accomplished negotiator, and could easily persuade the unwary that their shit was milk chocolate if he had half a consideration to do so. Bolstered by the wistful comfort of his Man-Made Mudman in Arctic fatigues, Chris reasoned that he'd do just swell, and if historical returns were anything on which to base a cheeky prognosis, he'd likely stumble upon a sexually malnourished cluster of buck wild teen savages who were keen to further their predominantly female species.

Having eluded several armed troops throughout his own mission, Chris became consequently downcast in the unwelcome role of prey. It appeared that local governments had covertly enlisted the aid of dozens of buckshee weekend-warriors in their efforts to diminish the number of free-roaming *whistlers* posing a threat to the country's resurgence. Eager to please their superiors, these have-a-go heroes were largely elated to be permitted the right to bear arms and stood fast against their appropriated enemy. Resigned to bedding down in derelict barns and such truck, Chris spent many a night tracing the arc of the moon through fractured windows, swathed in dewy blankets with little hope to buoy him through the night, and menaced by bubbles of obstinate snot that he hadn't the will to swab. Amid such episodes of dire melancholy, he reflected on their hasty decision to renounce the relative safety of Layten's Chute compound in favour of this hellacious excursion into this surreal and equally torrid version of no-man's land.

Chris "the cat" Harris had conquered many miles in his pilgrimage, this loveless expedition across the desolate in search of a utopian circumstance under which he'd lay his head without fear of brutal dictatorship leeching his ebbing vitality. A seemingly eternal Winter laid siege upon his cavalier heart, systematically eroding the gladsome character for which he was formerly celebrated and leaving a hollow and listless chaff stalking the realm in the name of liberty. The scuffed leather boots in which he shod his pallid trotters were most thoroughly saturated and chilled beyond any reasonable suggestion of comfort, and his teeth clicked as of a shorn bag snagged and pulled into rags, martyr to the gales and snapping evermore. In his sufferance, he recalled a remotely pertinent predicament in years past that had arisen from a quality of poor judgement and the careless application of shallow logic. He'd once been the proud owner of a delightful trike of strong yellow luminescence and was known to ride it about the south shore, knees pumping rhythmically as he rattled amid white picket fences and glorious tulips with bees agog. One fateful day, to his distaste, he'd slid through a batch of shrouded dogshit and accrued a ghastly reserve of reeking stripes upon his wheels. Loathe to risk an intimate contact with the foul, gelatinous compound, he'd thrown his trike into the sea, faithful that the ocean in its providential proximity would cleanse his adored mount and he'd be at liberty to ride again. Against his frugally calculated odds the water snatched greedily of his blow-moulded wheels, and though he endeavoured to reach it, it bobbed teasingly above dark and forbidding waters, such that could conceivably harbour an idling sea-beast with the express intention of clutching a skinny boy's ankles and gnawing at him with impractically long and sinister teeth. Flanked by a smattering of empathic chums, he watched as the ocean claimed his tricycle and all attempts to retrieve it became inconceivable. Then a speck upon the distant waves, he began to speculate confessing its loss to his mother, who would unquestionably *scud him across the lug* in consideration of his profound carelessness.

Though he couldn't be held entirely accountable for the world's spectacular downturn, Chris nonetheless lamented his extensive backlog of shit decisions and their undeniable impact on his pursuit of bliss. Mindfully respectful of fate, he was nominally reassured by the notion that whatever manner of casual abandon to which he'd tirelessly adhered, his higher purpose would one day emerge, and all pieces of the puzzle would seamlessly mesh.

Torn from his reflections by a cold, driving rain that made to pierce his flesh like a relentless volley of tiny arrows, his thrifted coat was whipped about his legs and for all the world he desired only to fall to the cracked and overgrown road, to be overwhelmed by a deep and pivotal fugue during which he'd be extracted from this world of protracted nightmares. Then, on the wind there came a human utterance as he walked his penance. Amid the swirling slices of dislodged signage that blew by, spinning throughout this autumnal vortex he heard a baby cry, and her voice rang destiny in its timbre. A phrase cuffed him upside the head, woven among the lilt and peal of this mysterious echo he discerned the words *I don't know if it matters.*

Forging on, he saw a house in the near distance, its portals roughly clad with boards.

The Cat Hits Back
(No-One Cares, Work Harder)

George "Geordie" Pop just couldn't digest the whole omnipresent advertising campaign behind *Peppy Cat* tuna flakes and associated enterprises, although he was clearly in a minority. Having grown up with cats in his house, he was kitty-cat-savvy, carrying zero animosity towards a feline presence and harbouring an enduring fondness for all their endearing quirks and characteristics. *Peppy Cat*, however, worried at him like the proverbial snarl of grit that galls at the most vulnerable spot of your whole foot, until you temporarily derail your entire program to sit the fuck down and pluck it out.

It wasn't the concept of brand characters that bothered him, as there were those he adored, but some fundamental aspect of Peppy Cat's integrity that ate him alive every time he switched on a television set, opened a magazine, or even walked by a bus shelter and dared to look up from his shoes for a moment. Before you even began to disassemble the campaign's retarded logistics and theory (surely an ambassador for the promotion of canned tuna should be indigenous to the ocean?), the poor, malformed and feckless oddity had a neck longer than Monday, and what cat needs that? Adding insult to injury, the final bruised and worm-ridden cherry on this entire colossal cupcake of baked human remains glazed in a layer of fresh shit was that every single can of Peppy Cat tuna contained a miniature edible Peppy Cat with the texture of cold aspic. With no additional expenditure incurred, *you too* could bite down on this superbly rendered jelly vision of *cat cool* as a supplement to your delicious fresh sandwich and side serving of kale.

"There goes Natasha. Whoops! *Nat forgot to feed the cat,*" went the jingle.

Geordie Pop switched off the television set, having resolved to do something less boring instead.

An obstinate fledgling writer of some blasphemously unorthodox fiction, he was no stranger to living frugally, and shared a communal apartment building with two other guys and a largely asexual irregularity named Brown. Brown, despite the glaring void that pretty dresses, ribbons and lipstick typically occupied, was not entirely unappealing, and her upbeat, personable approach to cooperative habitation was a frequent catalyst to Geordie Pop's bawdy imagination. The mere inference of her immaculate standing was sufficient to set his mind ablaze with ruminations of the sweetly dilating and unblemished cherries nestling beneath her thick, uncompromising pullovers; not to mention the idyllically soft fold from whence she might piss crystal waters. However, loathe to shake of their collaborative calm, Brown's hidden objects remained shrouded in secrecy and her status as the untouchable enigma retained its teasing dignity, irrespective of Pop's turgid urges.

His remaining strange bedfellows were an eclectic mix of largely unsympathetic gaiety, consisting of "Toy" Graham (so-called simply due to his diminutive stature loaning him the characteristics of a detailed miniature with which an infant might repose), and Craig "Woolly" Woollett, with whom he'd been remotely amiable since their early school years.

Although they'd traded no animosities, Geordie Pop could have taken Graham and his chronically ambitious musical leanings with a pinch of salt, being simply devoid of any curiosity with regards to each other's affairs and aspirations. And though such a politically incorrect hot potato would ne'er be given public forum, Graham's overtly Uranian propensities galled him on a primordial level, giving him the insufferable *irrits* and going so far as to quake his fundamental constitution, such that had led him to this unsavoury juncture.

Woolly, on the other hand, he had a great measure of fondness for, sharing an abundance of common interests including their passion for establishment-terrorising rock and roll, watching endless repeat showings of celebrated black comedies and a fondness for traditional Scotch comic strips; such that would typically appear in the fun section of Northern newspapers, even condescending to adopt several of their evocative catch phrases and regional terms into their daily exchange. Though, surprisingly, despite all their amicable banter and rallying wit, they fell consistently short of establishing any semblance of an intimate homosocial bond, maintaining an impersonal and rather socially distant relationship throughout their collegiate period and the spectacular decline of the western civilisation that followed. Perhaps a considerable impediment in their road to cementing a more robust and noteworthy friendship was Woolly's capacity for exaggeration, or rather his overwhelming tendency to spin the most farcical and unnecessary yarns of virtually unadulterated horseshit, and one such example was the shady case of Craig's ultramarine school shoes. During a short walk to school, and barely shy of their impending teens, Craig had easily convinced Geordie Pop that despite school regulations forbidding the wear of any coloured shoe other than grey or black, he was permitted the grace of ultramarine blue because they fell into a unique and uncelebrated category known as *razorhip*, due to the unique cut of their soles.

"Check that out, man," Craig had importuned, performing a brief jig during which his tread was displayed to maximum effect.

Though their youthful imaginations were generally awash with reflections of giant sea monsters, eight-bit video games and intergalactic war, Geordie Pop was nonetheless impressed by the brutally jagged moulding of Craig's chunky grooves and readily accepted the razorhip claim. On a lowly subconscious level, he envied Craig's seamlessly cool facility to rock the shit out of his blue *razorhips*, reluctantly acknowledging that they were, in fact, some *smooth* fucking shoes; and all because Craig talked shit like running water.

There came a day when the bedsit collective had arranged to see a band playing at the local arena. Naturally, expectations were optimistically high, and the general mood was one of whimsically frenzied anticipation. The hard rock outfit in question were named *The Platinum Ballista*, and in addition to their extensive back catalogue of consistently gale-force rock and roll, they were a byword for longevity, having negotiated almost thirty years of celebrity and all the complicated ego trips, narcotics and social disease that came along with the deal. Opening for the Ballistas were a rather more domestic effort by the name of *Animal Strap*, spearheaded by the deviant sexual carnivore and all-round party boy, Skeeter Young. An enthusiastic fan of both outfits, Geordie Pop was trying to eat, as it was his understanding that his liquor-drinking prowess would exhibit a whole lot more steel with a solid foundation of absorbent nutrients floating around in his fluttering guts. Providing a whole arsenal of tasty victuals, Peppy Cat Corporations brought not only delicious, moist tuna flakes to your table, but a wealth of ready-to-eat favourites such as the can of short-cut spaghetti that he currently stirred in dreadful expectation of the revolting feline mascot that he knew was lurking in the tomato-rich depths of his pasta.

"So, what about your new writing project?" Graham asked. "How's that coming along?"

"Aw, it's okay," said Geordie Pop. "I just wish I could get some recognition for the effort I'm putting into it."

"You must never give up," Graham condescended. "Before you know it, *your* name will be all over the TV. It might even supersede Poppy Cat."

"Yeah, thanks. And it's *Peppy Cat*," he returned, flashing Graham the kind of hollow smile that conveyed a deep-rooted and flagrant insincerity, sufficient to curl the hairs of his stupid gay moustache and beard that he stood preening whilst Geordie Pop wrangled with his cold spaghetti.

"Do we look like rock stars?" Graham asked of Craig.

"Yeah, look at me," Craig feigned. "I've got a one-room bedsit."

Aloof from the hum of conversation and derision among his unlikely housemates, Geordie Pop hooked a glistening blob of dark matter from what remained in his tin of rich spaghetti strands and turned it, that he might look upon the face of his self-congratulatory lampoon.

Peppy Cat's wide, bulging eyes regarded him with demure innocence, cradled on the fork's saucy tines, its neck canted evocatively in an expression of submissive allure, and Pop's stomach churned awhile, leaving him suddenly, inexplicably bilious. The cat was nothing but a cheap, gelatinous figurehead for a faceless corporation, and yet a cold, congealed affront to his confused sensibilities and stymied efforts toward an ambitious future.

Bastardising his fork to propel the cat into the wastepaper basket with schoolboy finesse, while enormously satisfying, would be to acknowledge his worsting; a submission to the guile and charm of an insignificant and slippery morsel that under normal circumstances would be bolted quicker than a bleb of errant phlegm.

Though it rippled of his soured belly to do so, he tucked the flaccid kitty into his mouth where it flounced upon his tongue and manifested as a shower of sickening things. It became a tangle of perch guts, torn from the tiny fish's mouth on a many-barbed hook during a Scottish camping trip when pubic hair was favoured. It smacked of a rude jar filled with a noxious infusion of cigarette-ends, farts and tap water; used as an amusing deterrent in the interests of kicking the foul habit. It was a juvenile mole, crushed beneath a bucket's lip by a graceless hand in the days of rubber keyboards and sexual awakening, silently pawing at the air in order to right itself, though its giblets were forced out through its anus and its bones very likely ground to a bloody dough.

Yet fully aware of the subterfuge and inventive fancies his subconscious mind supplied, Geordie Pop was halfway to believing that if he bit down on the jelly puss, he'd experience the full horror of its little bitty skull being smashed between the unrepentant might of his jaws, and the subsequent leaking of its tart brain behind his lips. An additional factor was the bogus snuffing of the benevolent creature's effervescence, the bringing of sleep to those undeserving of their premature eternal dark. Against a not inconsiderable natural repulsion he swallowed it whole, condemning the oily tidbit to being slowly churned and digested amid an unappetising soup of chewed whole-wheat spaghetti and an unrelenting tide of various lagers and reeking shots. And though the creature was gone, exiled to the inky, stinky blackness of Pop's digestive tract, it turned his belly bitter, each belch becoming a painfully acidic and pungent wrench of his poorly gut.

He swallowed the cat to staunch his ire.
Into the mire, its outlook was dire.
His tummy's a'fire.

Getting a whole bunch of tickets to see The Platinum Ballista had been a major coup for this ofttimes culturally apartheid bully bunch, and so regardless of acid reflux and the outside chance of a coincident *brown-trouser* manifestation, these crazy cats made it to the church on time and hearkened to the voice of visceral rock and roll gospel. *Got rock*? *Shock rock!*

Determined to express maximum enjoyment from the rare brush with rock royalty, Geordie Pop rolled as hard as he was able, despite the turmoil around his middle. He wondered, fleetingly, about what pertinent scientific theory there existed concerning rock shows and the pungency of malodour, as when someone farted at a gig, it was for real. Being something of a veteran on the regional rock scene, it occurred to him that such meteoric *trouser coughs* were typically rife therein, and that some elusive common factor was affecting their potency, elevating them to such a level as one could register their deeply offensive flavour. And if it weren't for clouds of effluence, then it was just as probable to arrive belly to back with the most nonchalant purveyors of an acrid body odour popular in the nineteen-eighties, and with crowd density preventing any immediate means of escape.

It was with measured jubilation, then, that Geordie Pop happened upon former acquaintance and celebrated sperm bank, Lacey Beenshill, decorated about her high cheekbones with shimmering glitter like a haunting, alluring green foxfire. It wasn't without credence to lose oneself within such pearlescent mist and belong to the spurious light's fervour, deigning to the mire 'mare beyond the veil that picked at the bones of men and stockpiled of their hearts and spirit.

Lacey was indeed beautiful, but possessed of a fearsomely unsavoury reputation, such that her cavernous gulley might be likened to opening a window and *hitt'n skins with the night*. For all her radiant glory, she appeared to be alone; starving at a feast, if you will, and Pop felt the characteristic draw that all red-blooded men experience in the face of such overt sexuality. Seeing little benefit in attempting to initiate a romantic fillip with the ever-shrouded Brown, he assumed a predatory perspective in favour of Beenshill, although the richer prize of Brown's elusive knockers would continue to provide insufferable fantasy for the term of his natural life. As it were, engaging in an obvious effort to seduce his strait-laced housemate would doubtlessly trigger the dawning of problematic social awkwardness within their camp, and the cat didn't want that.

"Hey, Lacey," he began, sidling close. "I never had you down as a rock n' rolla? More to the point, I don't think I ever got you down for the *third* time."

"Oh, hi, Geordie Pop," she lilted. "I can't listen to this trash, but it's the only time there's been something like a pulse in this old backwater swamp for months. Who's watching you?"

"Nobody. I'm with Woolly and Graham," he explained. "And you know Brown?"

"Oh, Toy Graham is such a sweetheart, isn't he?" she patronised. "Who's Brown?"

"You know that skirt from art classes and shit? The one with the glasses and all the thick jumpers."

"Oh, yeah," Lacey sneered. "What's up with her?"

"Nothin', I guess. She's around here somewhere."

"Well, where does she get off with all those sweaters and stuff?" asked Lacey. "And those glasses like the bottoms of soda-pop bottles? And her hair is just *there*, it doesn't *do* anything."

"Hey, she's okay," said Geordie Pop, a little too defensively. "She's just… ordinary."

"Ordinary?" Lacey questioned. "That's kinda another word for *plain*, isn't it?"

"Yeah, well. I didn't come over here to talk about her lack of fashion instinct," he said.

"So, what did you come to talk about, Sweetie?"

"Well, maybe I wasn't thinking about talking at all," he teased, pecking her perilously close to her perfect lips; a bold, brisk and feather-light gesture of his amorous aspirations.

"You feel like getting out of here?" she asked.

"Yeah, but maybe a few more songs," he trolled. "A couple more drinks."

Geordie Pop snaked an arm around her sumptuous waist, pulling her suggestively close to the little guy that stirred just below the breadbasket, her soft heat tangible below a layer of snagging sequins.

"Just who do you think you are?" Lacey feigned, a spark of inordinate triumph playing across her dark and unfathomably deep hazel eyes.

"I dunno, sweetness," he said, the eternal braggart. "Maybe some kind of god or something."

"Well," she hissed, playfully. "God came to the *wrong* town tonight,"

Too damn drunk and high on the prize in Lacey's eyes, Geordie Pop threw a cursory glance over the immediate crowd in search of the imperfects with whom he'd embarked on this musical mystery adventure. It appeared that (if not for his most recent acquaintance), he was totally alone in an ocean of faceless imitators; alone again, naturally.

Let us not beguile ourselves to assume that Lacey Beenshill was prepared to invest any emotional capital in this confused and wayward wastrel of a boy who was filled with a fabulous disaster of alcopop and misdirected frustration. This catastrophic coupling was merely a *borrowing* of opportune convenience, a peripatetic pairing in typical fashion of the throw-away society into which they were thrown.

No-one cares, work harder, urged the cat beneath his fat. For even the unbiased and fully inhibited Brown had cast off; had relinquished the threads under which their odd acquaintance had previously floundered, perhaps idling on a thermal current of provisional rebellious abandon, all social disparities temporarily rescinded. With a sneer of punk attitude, Geordie Pop departed the hall of rock and roll fame, leaving the sweating, laughing student-types and generic mallcore army to satisfy their own unremarkable aspirations, scrabbling around amongst the discarded ticket stubs and smashed beer cups for guitar picks and the like; mementoes of an evening they'd otherwise forget, being neck-deep in a dangerous blend of *meow meow* and other such desperate glimpses of a world preferable to theirs.

"I guess they'll realise I've gone when the taxi fare's gone up by a third," he lamented.

Arriving at the hulking old run-down Victorian terrace that Lacey then called home, Pop was suffused by the realisation that this was probably one of those nights which developed into the kind of wild ride you still talked about years later, layering on non-functional details as and when preferred because you were surrounded by faux friends you'd only just met. Fortified with an unexpected sexual tension, they fumbled their way upstairs, clumsily negotiating the wide, creaking staircase after necking on the doorstep for a considerable interval, grabbing soft handfuls of one another's indelicate quarters and bringing about some measure of fine discharge. It was at that juncture that things developed a rather alarmingly surreal cast, and our unfortunate hero became subject to a most irregular season of events.

Imbued with low-grade liquor and a dusting of heavily *bashed* narcotic, Geordie Pop thought little of being ushered into a shadowy bedroom and manoeuvred onto some fashion of deeply padded table, availed of the realisation that he and the deviant Lacey were not alone. So dense were the shadows (and by the same token, so sparse the filtered moonlight), that he could not discern from whence the giggling voices came until his entire focus was appropriated by the naked form of blonde Kerry.

"Kerry will take care of you," Lacey declared from the depths of murk. "Kerry, take good care of him."

Lost for words, his clothes seemed to simply evaporate, and he was laid helplessly bare beneath this warm, slender pixie with titties like little cupcakes, jiggling with her every movement as she assumed the dominant position, stoking fire in Pop's abdomen and melting his brain with animal avidity. Struck from a markedly different mould to Lacey, who was concurrently preoccupied with some undisclosed sapphic conspirator, Kerry was nonetheless attractive; wide-eyed and willowy, of an elfin stamp. But, for the grace of fortune should she retain a dour and phlegmatic carriage, because her smile betrayed a mouth bristling with the most aggressively misaligned and serrated teeth that soured her otherwise delectable appeal. Surely with such a viciously jagged arrangement of buckled incisors and canines, she'd not be deterred from chewing through barriers of sheet steel to fulfil an appointment of fair import; although largely indifferent to her unsettling deformity, Geordie Pop was firing on all cylinders, and reached down 'twixt her hairless cleft to assess developments in the field. Ploughing around the nub of her distended clitoris, he was duly astounded by the magnitude of her dewy flow, and following a brief, exploratory caress of her hole, steered his *little Pop* into the deliciously sopping heat, his mind agog with a creeping sensation of cosmic ecstasy permeating his whole body, and then it was gone.

Yet taken with a mindless lust for this superlatively imperfect creature, he grabbed at her tiny, flouncing breast, quivering in its sweating magnificence as she rode him. In his reckless fervour, his rough hands squeezed of the soft, resilient egg as if to kill it, pinching her turgid nipple.

"You're hurting me," she snapped. "Not so hard, you arsehole!"

A tad bit harsh, considering their fortuitous intimacy, Geordie Pop considered, and a perfect storm manifested therefrom. As he persisted in fornication, nonetheless affected by the callous rhetoric, he was flipped from her dripping gash by manner of surplus oil and began to soften like a fat slug.

With scarcely a sigh of derision, his odd mistress left the table and was duly gathered among the shadows, consumed by suspiciously loud, wet kisses and baffled chuckles. Her graceful ghost was enveloped by the barely perceptible mounds of yielding flesh writhing together in an outrageously climactic knot, indifferent to his plight as he lay nude on a rudimentary altar, legs parted in a V. *Just like that*; the *confounded* cat.

Geordie Pop reposed in a small pool of lady's drizzle, entirely discombobulated and unsure of what would be considered the conventional strategy during which to elope, all the while chafed by a repetitive verse filtering through the bare boards below.

Bears, boars and snow; the laired wolves we know, leading fat flies and crows. *I only wanna dream when I'm with you*, the track echoed.

Stranded in the shadowed chamber, feeling quite rejected.

The lowly form of Geordie Pop was thoroughly dejected.

Scholastically, an average pupil, which his grades reflected.

This kid had never been so broken down and disconnected.

With an enforced surge of gung-ho resolve, he finally rose and set about dressing himself, and seeing little benefit to projecting a facade of quietude and subtlety, faced the mangle of grinding, sucking, tricksy sluts, allowing that his bobbing member swung its pendulous, judgemental arc in their direction as he readied himself to leave. Nary a syllable was exchanged as he snatched his leather jacket from a chair and took his grudging leave of a room filled with a tantalising pile of glorious brown teats, bags of pliant skin and dribbling, salty cavities from which he'd been practically black-balled.

From the general vicinity of the monotonous, morose and malfeasant track that had so badly nettled him, Geordie Pop detected the raucous tones of merriment and a suggestion of celebration upon descending the beaten staircase. Faced with an alternative that consisted of making his way shamefully home with only the bitter tang of humiliation and non-acceptance on his lips, he decided that a brief investigation shouldn't be too great a risk of his remaining honour.

As it transpired, he and Lacey had unwittingly infiltrated an impromptu party that appeared to be spearheaded by a local *shit-heel* named Sam Sidney, whose less than respectable credentials included a penchant for drugs and rumours of an incestuous bearing. Since Lacey was out of the picture and presumably no longer a pertinent factor, Geordie Pop was faced with the unenviable prospect of relating a tale of lost pride to his housemates upon his return, and therefore felt it imperative that he party this out, taking maximum advantage of an opportunity for a few precious grains of personal redemption.

Then such an inglorious boon was it that he realised the presence of Angèle Pandy, for whom he'd carried a fluttering torch just shy of a decade; and making whose acquaintance would surely bolster his flagging self-regard, providing him with sufficient material to weave a more fortunate account to relay to his housemates. Angèle was no more French than she was homosexual, and despite Geordie Pop's questionable bouquet, seemed genuinely pleased to see him peeking through the battle-scarred portals into a room predominantly populated by strangers. Though relatively short of stature, she was an exquisite creature of the most breathtaking symmetry, and one that Geordie Pop had previously admired from afar, regarding her to be quite beyond the means of his social orbit. Her perfect lips were like a flower, enticing and resplendent in their delicate, flawlessly natural intricacies, and her eyes burned with a piercing clarity; the pure, depthless pearlescence a consummate contrast to their near-black counterpart. Although keen to take full advantage of a gifted opportunity, he was under no misconception that this transcendent beauty would, under normal circumstances, be out of his league, her effortless appeal the bitter envy of the female scholastic fraternity during their schooldays.

"Sit with me!" she demanded, scooting aside the hulking, floral armchair that cradled her like an infant.

"Don't have to tell me twice," said Geordie Pop. "I take it this is Sam's party. Can I get a beer?"

"You can have mine," she said, handing him a yellow tin. "I think I've had enough already."

"What makes you say that?" he asked.

"My knickers are right up my arse," she announced.

"And that's beer-related?" He joked. "Thank you for the information."

As they laughed together in relaxed and joyful abandon, he applied little effort to repressing the image of an elaborate rope of twisted black lace applying unwelcome friction to her stately undercarriage; a far cry from the sawtooth swamp pig he'd recently laboured beneath.

Leaning in to chance his arm with a tentative and experimental kiss, he was enamoured by her radiant beauty, spellbound by the realisation of imminent contact with those chiselled, exquisite lips. The commotion within his sweating bosom was likened to the clamour and squall of a flock of seagulls, suddenly taking to the skies in rapid parody of one another. This was more than sufficient to the most basic expectations of Geordie Pop, who in that moment would proclaim to rescind all prospects and worldly possessions in favour of a pastoral existence spent reflecting on that time he necked with Angèle Pandy. Savouring in this amorous transference of their particulate grace, he knew emancipation from all things within his personal nirvana; suffused by her youthfully exuberant exhalations in the chaotic jungle of a low-grade student accommodation. Stars lit up in his head and great moons collided, but he was loathe to pay court to further intimacies lest biological evidence of his previous liaison with that unfortunately bohemian dropship (whose name he hadn't cared petition) be uncovered.

"I like the way we mistreat love," he said in vain.

"So go ahead and use me," she suggested.

Geordie Pop stared into her dark crystal eyes with their flecks of sparkling jet, secretly wishing that the likes of Woolly Craig or even Graham had been around to hear the widely coveted Angèle Pandy request that he use her, and thereby immortalising the exclusive moment for as long as they all should live. The tasteless decision of whether to venture exposing such a preciously flirtatious object of widespread desire to his filthy cock was taken mercifully from his hands as the evening began its raucous and unrestrained descent into entropic mayhem. The intangible, yet nonetheless spiritual fusion their eyes beheld was irreparably broken and dispersed as a portion of the bulkhead adjacent to the hall was destroyed and dragged crashing to the drawing room floor amid the choking form of Sam Sidney, who'd been performing pull-ups in a voluminous cotton shirt.

"Fuck it." He coughed. "It's rented. I can send it back."

No sooner had the clouds of aged and dusty plaster settled upon the rugs, congesting the hall with clusters of broken wood and shreds of Deco wallpaper, than a noisome disturbance hailed their collective attentions from outside; specifically the assemblage of parked cars in no particular order. What's occurring throughout this ugly procession of tin-pot vehicles? This arbitrary collection of rusted fenders and bald tyres, flashing lights and reeking footwells concealing all manner of tack, from half-eaten burgers dotted with ambling ants to domestic-level narcotics and oversized coins that could no longer ready player one in any respectable emporium on the north-east coast of the Spanish city.

Vandalism was occurring, as a prelude to grand theft auto.

"Hey, Sam," bayed a curious onlooker. "They're fucking up your car,"

The vast and outmoded drawing room featuring en suite kitchen and dinette rapidly assumed a vehement jumble of pounding feet and fallen glass bottles, the congregation rushing for the door in the hope of bearing witness to Sam's vengeful measures with regards to the indignity of mutilations upon his tiny effeminate car. Entirely indifferent, Geordie Pop enjoyed his proximity to the statuesque Angèle, whilst quaffing contentedly from his yellow tin that featured a bear motif.

"Shouldn't we call the police?" she suggested.

"Someone will," said Geordie Pop. "Let's not get involved."

From beyond the obscurity of the partially draped and considerable bay window, under the murky glow of the tall lamps and between driven clouds of pellet-like snow there arose a commotion of foul tongues and cries of anguish, accompanied by an almost tribal beating of living bones on lacquered panels and the inevitable bursts of shattered glass. After a short time, as the disgruntled cries of promised retribution for inconveniences incurred in the name of frontier justice faded into the distance, punctuated by random acts of further vandalism intended to embody outraged defiance and the onset of an undying cycle of punitive violence, Sam and his buckshee entourage filtered back into the house, aglow with their landslide victory over the unruly clutch of young bucks who'd fancied their chances of something for nothing. Flushed with pride, Sam the fat bastard recounted his brave foray into the hordes of usurpers and the unjust, his single beetling eyebrow performing a comically animated ripple relative to his regrettable exuberance. Naturally, his intimate troop of freeloading, parasitical simpletons hung on his every word; for he was indeed the unbalanced son of an incestuous rapist, and despite an underlying heart condition, his petulant outbursts were well documented.

This pseudo-soiree settled into its former groove of extrovert machismo and lecherous liaison; the sweating, steaming apes revelling in their alpha capacities at the top of this recently established pile, until presently there came a rapping at the door, as of many skeletons begging emancipation from their insufferably overcrowded closet. Overwhelmed by the dissonant din of party tapes and outspoken vulgarities, the tattoo boomed to an alarming crescendo, cracking the pane of opaque glass, and eventually splitting the aged pine to permit the infiltration of a maddened Scotch conglomerate, their feet encrusted with dirty snows.

A freezing wind announced the advent of this uninvited herd, the likes of which rarely heralded the arrival of glad tidings and wishes of prosperity for a glittering year ahead. Heads turned and loud, phlegmatic cacklings were reduced to a hushed whisper as the thuggish detail took centre stage, mere inches from the comfortable armchair shared by Geordie Pop and Angèle Pandy. Assuming the altogether ostentatious role of responsible spokesperson and fat controller, Samuel Sidney stood forward to address the house.

"Can I help you?" he asked of them, his body language throwing down a gauntlet forged from unalloyed arrogance and self-gratification.

"Who beat up my brother?" rasped the foremost unshaven Scot. "He's fighting for his life."

"He was lively enough when he ran off," Sam replied. "After trying to steal my car."

"I take it you're the ringleader? This your house?" the Scotch captain demanded, raising his apish, leather-clad arms to better stipulate the house and contents.

"I live here, yeah," said Sam.

"Well, this is our house now," announced the Scot. "And if there's no' a cold beer in that fridge for me, we're not just gonna kick the shit out of you, we're gonna fucking *kill* you."

Visibly discomposed, Sam's eyes darted every which way in appraisal of his own outfit; specifically how it measured up in comparison to this brutish grunge assembly of a speculative eight scoffing at his authority.

"You can't chill here," Sam replied. "You need to wrap your shit up."

"You say that like you have any kind of credibility around here anymore." The Scot smirked. "You're having a nightmare, pal."

At this damning proclamation the Scotch orator closed the gap on Sam's last stand, and flanked by a body of menacing, fearsome goons, commandeered his unimpressive physical form, manhandling him out onto the winter road that they might augment his beatings with greater efficiency. It should be noted that during the coup, although outwardly affronted by the permissive expropriation of their illustrious leader, none took the floor to manifest their displeasure; nor did any sanguine individual incite to confess umbrage with the marauding Scots. In the more customary terms recognised by the laymen concerned in this cautionary tale, everyone took it royally in the ass.

Wild winds cut through the previously warm and comfortably ignoble ambience of this contentious seat of learning, and the occasional speck of hail danced through the tiled hall, only to melt amid fallen lumber and crumbs of plaster like the hearts and volitions of our cowed men. The music played on, insofar as drinking continued subtly and quietly under the baleful glare of the remaining highlanders, and while Sam's practically defenceless hull received a frightful drubbing, awash with slush and his own crimson fret. After a time the aggressive Scot returned, accompanied by stooges grafted in his own image; and although there was no sign of fat Sam, his absence wasn't queried, and nobody rushed to attend his projected wounds or telephone the emergency services to detail their *banjoed* friend. Fear for their own cowardly hides subdued the trembling sheep, quelling any propositions of revolt against the machine.

"Now," began the Scot, his cheeks aglow from December's kiss. "Where's that fuckin' beer?"

Following the barbarous indecency of Samuel's good hiding, a new party evolved from the former's ashen remains, and although it numbered fewer, its steadfast celebrants were altogether sombre and coltish. For the vengeful Scots it was a free bar, a warm hearth, and the sheer metaphorical joy of drinking a frothing draught from the skulls of their defeated enemies. In view of the potential violence threatening their plumply pink, formerly easy-going and cocksure meat-suits, Samuel's subjugated troops nibbled conservatively of their defrosted profiteroles and sipped supermarket lager while their Scotch aggressors rode the wind, forever free.

Through passage of time the occasional, spirited detainee would succeed in slipping the defences and making good their escape into the bracing Winter night, until few but the ill-fated form of Geordie Pop remained, having ushered the beautiful Angèle and her twisted underpants to eventual liberation during a group rendition of some classic skinhead number that approximated a powerful upright vacuum cleaner beset by glass marbles.

Such was Geordie Pop's forsaken disposition that he considered the likelihood of invisibility, as the marauders paid him no mind, leaving him alone to nurse his yellow tin that had been warm and empty for what seemed like hours whilst reflecting on his unenviable predicament. In this barely tolerable climate of social alienation he pondered the fates of the coven by whose misappropriation he'd wound up beached on an armchair and shivering like a shitting dog despite the room's muggy ambience. As it were, he cared little for the fortunes of Lacey, *Shovelmouth* and the unknown vessel (probably something basic like Louise), or whether they were aware of the evening's furore, huddled upstairs in their deviant little polyamorous triad; aloof to poor, irritant Sam having the living shit kicked out of him by the modern equivalent to William Wallace.

After all's said and done, whosoever cared for Geordie Pop, deeply and dangerously alone? *Not I*, said the cat. *He's a braggart and a brat.*

The boisterous highlanders looked to be having immense fun at the student household's expense, prompting him to review the merit of the Scot's story regarding a sibling in intensive care, for what it mattered. This was a clean-cut example of control and oppression, and a very tenuous case of justifiable retribution if ever there was one. On those grounds, and the lightly held supposition that he was of such fleeting import to the Scotch consortium that he could simply walk away unscathed, he fixed to abscond. Once beyond the influence of this particularly sapping circle of hell he'd run like the wind and never speak of it again; or at least until the keenness of its terrifying grip had diminished to the extent that his shite less resembled a hot, uncomfortable goulash over which he held fragile dominion. Providing further encumbrance to the evening's considerable tally of uncharitable transgressions and revelations, it appeared that his well-loved leather jacket had been blown adrift, its pockets laden with such essential items as keys, a loaded wallet and his electric telephone. So overwhelming had been the storm of ardour surrounding the long-coveted taste of Angéle Pandy's sweet oyster that he'd been oblivious to the coat's transgression; and though he was marginally confident that he'd wrested it from the bizarre and bitterly disenchanting boudoir above stairs, he'd no recollection of its machinations since then.

Geordie Pop stood shakily on legs riddled with prickling paresthesia, concurrently wroth by his own cowardice in the face of urban tyranny and nevertheless inspired, for he alone had dined on cold spaghetti and jelly cat.

"Have you seen my jacket?" he enquired of a surly character, whose coordination was evidently awry in correlation with the level of diabolic moonshine in the thick bottle he carried.

"What would I want with your jacket?" the guy sneered. "I got my own fucking jacket."

"Oh, yeah," fluttered Geordie Pop. "My mistake."

"Hey!" shouted the bottle guy in an expedient bid for the attention of his peers. "This dude's saying that we stole his jacket."

From the incredible invisible man and non-intrusive onlooker to a focal point of the entire sordid venue in one effortless stroke, Geordie Pop back-pedalled fit to burst his breeches.

"Nah, that's not what I was suggesting," he softly protested. "I just wanted my jacket. So I could leave, you know?"

"You'll leave when we say you can leave," rebuked the original Scot, regaining prominence as the overall delegate and foremost protein-boss. "Who are ye? This *your* house?"

"No, I don't live here," he explained. "I was just... visiting."

"Visiting who?" the Scot wanted to know. "That fuckin' fat drink o' water we just pestled outside?"

"N-no," stammered Geordie Pop. "No, a girl."

"And where's your girl now?" the Scot demanded. "I don't have one, see? And there's a rule in our gang, that if you've got somethin', ye share it. Ain't that right boys?"

Smit by an emphatic cheer with the intended constitution of an affirmative return, Geordie Pop appeared incontestably beat, and began speculating as to whether he'd be acquitted the death penalty in favour of a near-fatal beating, the likes of which would undoubtedly deplete his waning effervescence.

"We're here to do the devil's business," the Scot proclaimed, and hooking a hand around Geordie Pop's stiffly anxious neck, butted him on the crown, inducing a rather comically incongruous noise like that of two considerable pebbles colliding, their finish smooth and unimpeded.

The poor, unfortunate Geordie Pop was stunned as the highlanders fell in with booted kicks and punches, quickly flooring him and subsequently raining hell about his toppled mass. Acting on the deduction that resistance would be an exercise in futility, and that retaliation could conceivably result in either death, or an unappealing synthesis of broken bones and perforated organs, he curled himself into a fetal position in the hope that the blows would be largely absorbed by the meatier portions of his thighs and shoulders. His chin tucked into his chest, Geordie-Pop spirited away to a happy place to await such a time as the vicious Scots would grow weary of digging their bootheels into his thorax, or beaning him with glass bottles and simply disperse, appeased with their savage exploitations.

As the attack eventually slowed and he dared to squint through the one eye that still opened without the application of his trembling fingers, he fought to oppose the swirling black clouds fringed with sparkling flecks that threatened to overwhelm his consciousness and lull him into further peril. In this condition of dire incapacitation he was loathe to assess the resultant damage for fear of what horrors might be uncovered in addition to the evident *code brown* in his trousers, for during the agitation the Scots had engendered a colonic shame.

"I think we've established a pecking order here now," said the top Scot. "I do believe he's come around to our way of thinking."

The notion was concurred by his neanderthal clutch of grease-monkey goons, and as if the ill-fated Geordie Pop hadn't suffered sufficient indignities in the last ten minutes, a measure of *hockling* ensued, during which his shitty pants were supplemented with an unseemly gale of mucoid intrusions.

"Your jacket's in the backyard. Get the fuck out of here," the Scot grimaced. "You fuckin' stink."

Though beaten and disgracefully humiliated above all reasonable expectations, Geordie Pop was both relieved and grateful to be permitted his freedom, and absently speculated as to whether the intolerable cunt Samuel Sidney had been shown similar mercy. It was education indeed to be a party to such a blanket instance of averted eyes and spurned responsibility as he dragged his own smashed cadaver through a smattering of regretful overlookers; their primary concerns being personal anonymity and the survival of this wretched debacle. Ironically, he had scant justification to support such a staggering moral contradiction as to anticipate alms, as he'd joined hands with the silent during fat Sam's (albeit justifiable) birching.

Through the towering aperture of the kitchen door there blew a most refreshing balm of crisp, clean air, and though it carried a chilling flavour of the Arctic, it assured his freedom through nuances of open spaces and rural trends. Perhaps symbolic of a further misplaced irony, that upon tugging his bruised and barely functional legs over the stoop he was passed by a curious tabby, enticed by the comforting warmth from which he currently scrambled. Favouring him with a mechanically inquisitive sniff, it scampered into the house in pursuit of opportunistic indulgence, displaying as much concern for his fate as he'd conveyed to the gelatin rendition that melted in his stomach.

Tossed amid the crusted filth tainting the rear yard of this working-class residential pile, Geordie Pop found his jacket as the objectionable Scot had promised. Stiff with frost and layered with snow, it was something of an anchor to his previously free and easy existence, and he wrapped its sodden leather abundance about his shoulders before checking the pockets. Due in no small part to recent vexations, his mind was a kaleidoscopic vortex of fleeting emotions and half-remembered affairs, and his memories of carried stock were consequently vague. Alas, it seemed that he'd been looted during the odd transgressions and every pocket was bare, leaving him to endure the discomfiting spur of understanding that one or more of those egregious bastards from whom he'd freshly eloped was probably enjoying the free luxury of any drug paraphernalia or handfuls of loose change that might have nestled therein. Having long acknowledged the bitter, undisputable truth that there'd be precious little glory salvaged from this abortive excursion to Poortown, Gomorrah, population 13, he urged what middling zest remained under his volition to animate his brutally maltreated legs and made off into the alley, far from the buzz of remedial rock and roll and the thump of cavorting punks.

Once over the threshold of the unremarkable terrace to which Lacey Beenshill had so ingenuously led him what seemed like a lifetime ago, Geordie Pop had imagined he'd be safe from antagonism, the likes of which had stripped him of his dignity by means of tooth and nail. In the alley behind the house, surrounded by dustbins, feral cats and broken Christmas toys were the kind of unscrupulously bland, second-rate groupies that hadn't quite made it onto the metaphorical guest list, but were resolved to indulge beyond the invisible barrier of social hierarchy, come rain or shine. Hopeful that one or more of their social betters would deign to invite them inside, they partied in the freezing wasteland amid fat rats and smashed trash; drinking contentedly from huge plastic containers filled with improvised moonshine, reclining on chunks of salvaged furniture and flouting their questionable virtue in any old backyard with a neglected gate. Upon Geordie Pop's underwhelming intrusion into their seedy and deplorable sphere of influence, they were damnably curious as to the origins of this dishevelled and snow-topped boy whose odour smacked of fresh shit. Conversely, his wounded heart sank at the visage of these crew-cut and bare-butt sluts wearing hastily home-made t-shirts that depicted scenes of the crucifixion and names of various bands affiliated with violence and anarchic crime.

"What the fuck are you supposed to be?" a tall, imposing girl demanded of him.

Time and again throughout his relatively short span of existence, Geordie Pop had been the unenviable perpetrator of misplaced sarcasm and vitriolic lip, and so thorough was his malaise at this revolting convergence of events that he was past the point of all rational judgement, and indeed any responsible will for self-preservation.

"That's rich coming from you," he muttered. "You look like you're off to ruin a science fiction wedding, you cunt."

To his credit, this broad-shouldered amalgamation of the punk/skinhead subcultures displayed a heavy resemblance to many a skeletal anti-hero from fantasy-based cartoons and lucrative stop-motion productions alike; although his brash assessment of her image held room for improvement in terms of presentation, tact, and overall suitability.

Having been smartly denounced by this strange and debilitated shrew of a boy under the watchful eyes of her motley crew of post-nuclear bandits, the girl was reasonably incensed and keen to re-establish her prominence, lest she be reminded of this humiliation during polite conversation, and snatching a fistful of his unseemly hair, she twisted his gaze to meet hers in a vengeful gesture of urban domination.

"Ouch, you *bastard*," Geordie Pop hissed, lacking the active fibre to improve his standing.

"Who are you calling a bastard?" she retorted. "Here, you stink! Have you trodden in something?"

From his uncomfortable vantage point he gazed into her bright eyes, alight with reflections of the vivid moon and the alley's archaic lamps; therein he witnessed a buried beauty, wilfully sullied by popular direction of its own useless generation. Behind the mask of closely cropped hair, thick applications of theatrical makeup in black, urgent strokes and a vulgar, generic attitude sympathetic to the downtrodden and repressed there lurked a pretty girl with a checkable history of shit decisions, much like his own.

"Nah," he replied, softly. "I've shit myself a short while ago, but."

Her immediate response was one of brief and troubled bewilderment, permitting Geordie Pop the opportunity to ogle her exemplary titties; not entirely unsurprising considering their imposed proximity. Veiled in soft, white cotton, like her pretty eyes they were a somewhat vital reminder of her femininity, and his lurid adulations traced their almost geometrically infallible contours beneath stencilled slogans of antidisestablishmentarianism and war. Although her adopted temperament betrayed intentions of malice, these pockets of inconstant softness beguiled the poor, unfortunate Geordie

Pop and he wanted to kiss her, gradually milking the filth and fury from her potty mouth.

"Oh, you fucking rotter!" she exclaimed. "What's wrong with you?"

"I dunno, maybe it's a medical condition," he answered. "How you gonna kick the shit out of me now, eh?"

Predictably vexed, this caustic Bromley mouthpiece smartly dashed his already beaten dome against a telegraph pole, under whose shadow they shimmered like warring lovers beneath the stars.

Sparks flared behind his eyes and the flavour of a spoiled orange coursed over his bleeding gums on impact with the structure, yet the depth of his melancholic indifference was such that his tongue would not for a moment be stilled.

"Is that the best you've got?" Geordie Pop hissed. "Your Mum hit me harder than that on Christmas Eve. And she honestly did."

Teeth flashed and claws slashed on receipt of his eloquent and definitive curtailment, and his head was struck upon the giant beam with a rage and regularity fit to concuss his unborn children. Dislodging fair tufts of his matted hair, this skeletal punk swung the listless, afflicted infidel onto the rough cobbles of the lane, from whence he could now supplement his list of ailments with a nasty case of gravel-rash. Having finally piqued the interest of her rotten contingent, another belting began in earnest.

Semi-consciously preoccupied in the absorption of said belting, Geordie Pop was accorded a lucid moment during which the reality of manslaughter broke upon his sensibilities like yolk from a ruptured egg. Surprisingly, though his life so far could be likened to *shit-tip* or *inglorious catastrophic abortion*, he uncovered a rather passionate desire to fulfil it, and certainly not to undergo its conclusion at the hands of these maladjusted space-bandits whose appearances were reminiscent of running through a charity clothes shop coated in industrial contact adhesive.

At the end of the lane was a cluster of illuminated bollards and such truck, the express purpose of which was a semblance of traffic control within this densely populated area, and it was on this bewitching beacon of light that he both focussed his escape and fought the tantalising inclination to slip into a grave unconsciousness. Hauling himself towards the glow by means of badly skinned elbows and similarly shredded forearms, he performed an urban bastardisation of a sniper crawl, marginally palliated by the deficit these creatures owed the infernal highlanders in terms of ferocity and overall power. As the realisation that this nightmarish episode and all of its appallingly iniquitous excursions could be concluding, and that he might soon be licking his wounds at home with a multilevel showstopper of a story to relate to his previously sedate housemates, his aggressors appeared to lose interest and relieved their battery. Geordie Pop slackened his retreat accordingly, and as he did so, caught a point-perfect kick that sailed between his crumpled legs to quake the very nuclei of his reproductive organs; perhaps the singular portion of his body that had, up to this point, enjoyed amnesty.

"Dash it," he squeaked. "I do believe you've caught me in the sweetbreads."

"Fucking pervert," she retorted, and regrouped amid backslapping and jeers.

Geordie Pop was free, in the sense that he could now make his way home without risk of incursion, although on doing so he was handed a homespun flyer by an excitable young man, desensitised to the turbulent streets and perversions therein. The flyer advertised THE FALL, a revolutionary dropout society scheme in which one could enjoy a world of lawless survival at the uncomplicated cost of everything you'd ever known.